W9-ACP-761

THE SIX-DAY HERO

THE SIX-DAY HERO

Tammar Stein

KAR-BEN PUBLISHING
A division of Lerner Publishing Group, Inc.
241 First Avenue North
Minneapolis, MN 55401 USA
1-800-4-KARBEN

Website address: www.karben.com

Cover and interior images: © art-siberia/Deposit Photos (face); © iStockphoto.com/GeorgePeters (soldier silhouette); © iStockphoto.com/Vectorig (cat silhouette); © Veronica Wools/Dreamstime.com (eucalyptus tree); © Laura Westlund/Independent Picture Service (maps).

Main body text set in Bembo Std Regular 12.5/17.
Typeface provided by Monotype Typography.

Library of Congress Cataloging-in-Publication Data

Names: Stein, Tammar, author.
Title: The six-day hero / by Tammar Stein.
Description: Minneapolis, MN : Kar-Ben Publishing, [2017] | Includes bibliographical references.
Identifiers: LCCN 2016008962 (print) | LCCN 2016034159 (ebook) | ISBN 9781512458718 (lb : alk. paper) | ISBN 9781512428568 (pb : alk. paper) | ISBN 9781512428575 (eb pdf)
Subjects: LCSH: Israel-Arab War, 1967—Juvenile fiction. | CYAC: Israel-Arab War, 1967—Fiction. | Heroes—Fiction. | Israel—History—1948-1967—Fiction.
Classification: LCC PZ7.S821645 Si 2017 (print) | LCC PZ7.S821645 (ebook) | DDC [Fic]—dc23

LC record available at https://lccn.loc.gov/2016008962

Manufactured in the United States of America
1-41532-23367-5/6/2016

Dear Ima:

This book was your idea, and
I wrote it for you. I miss you.

Israel at time of the Six-Day War: June 1967

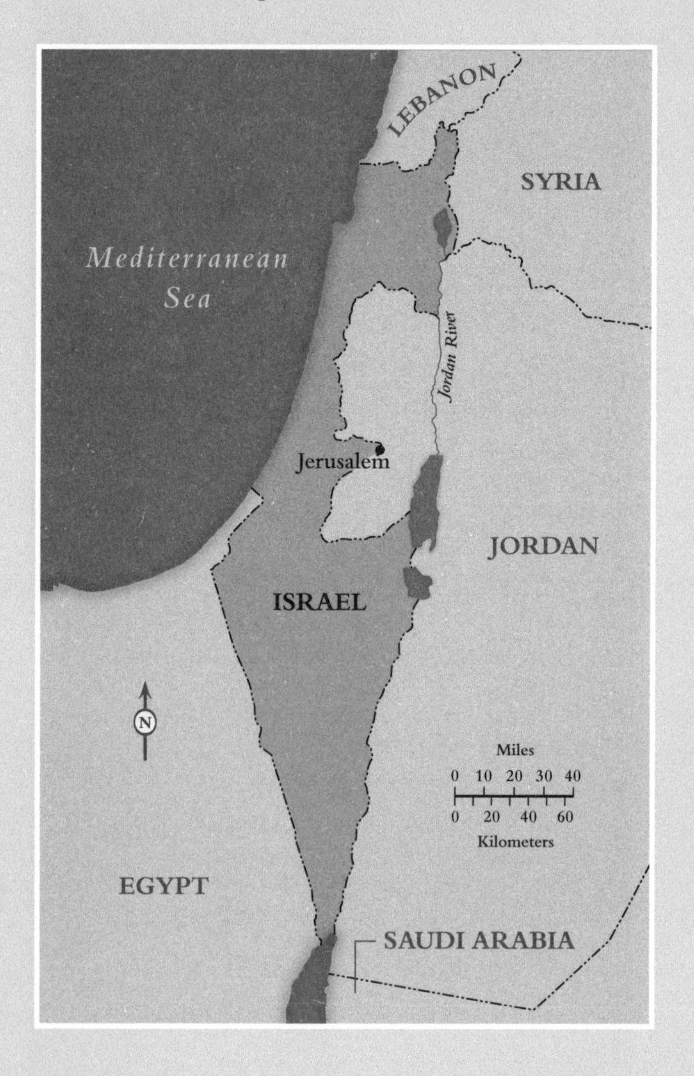

Jerusalem during the Six-Day War: June 1967

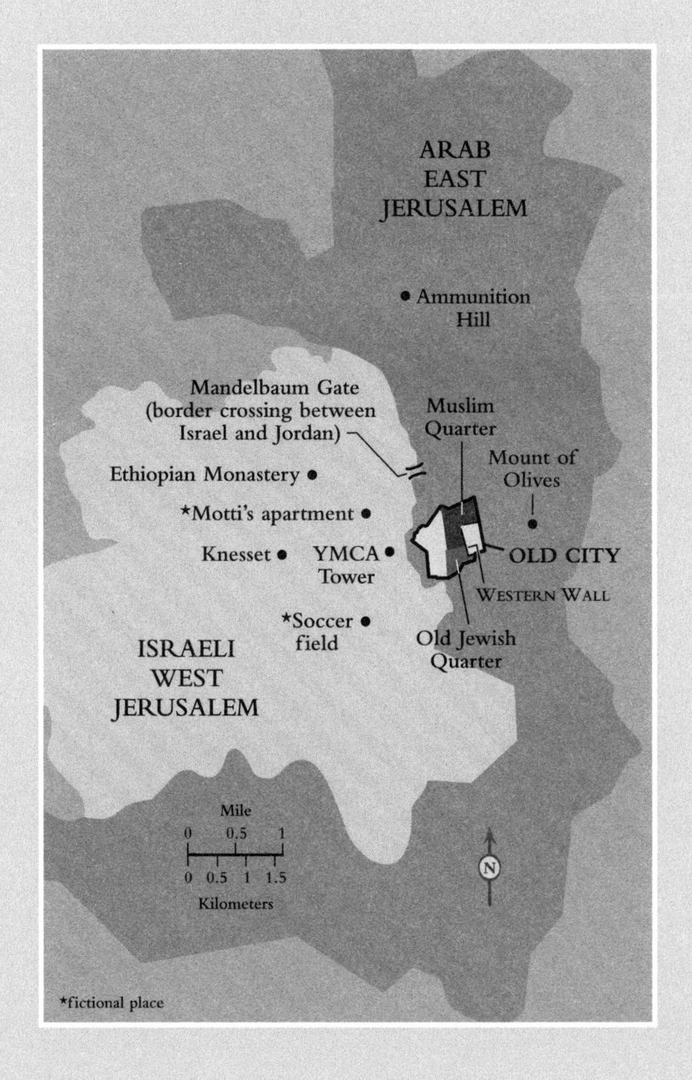

Before

We think we know the future. And we do, to some degree. Not what kind of job we'll have when we're grown. But tomorrow. Or next week. We know what's coming. School. Friends. Chores. The usual. We really believe that what happened yesterday is probably going to happen again today.

Except sometimes we're completely wrong.

In 1967, the world thought the Middle East was fine. The American president was briefed: there won't be another war for at least four years. In my country, Israel, the prime minister and his cabinet said the same: the situation looked okay. Nothing threatened our existence.

No one predicted what the month ahead would have in store for all of us.

Even the smartest people in the world can be wrong.

Part I
The Wait

Chapter One
Independence Day

I hate ceremonies. My dad knows this, of course. I catch him glancing over at me. He's got that look: half-annoyed, half-worried. I can't help squirming in my seat and jiggling my feet. Everyone sitting on our bench vibrates slightly. My dad places a heavy hand on my leg. I stop jiggling. I don't have a great record where formal events are concerned.

The president of Israel, Zalman Shazar, drones on.

My older brother, Gideon, is up on the stage, five people over from the president at the lectern. Gideon doesn't look bored. Like all the other Independence Babies—Israelis born on the same day as our country's independence day—he wears his olive-green Class A uniform. There are two hundred of them up on the stands. Today is their nineteenth birthday. Israel's nineteenth birthday too.

"Our country is strong," our president says. "Our country is growing . . ." Blah, blah, blah. I tune out the rest. Gideon looks fascinated.

"Abba," I hiss.

My dad looks over, annoyed.

"I gotta piss."

His lips press together in a tight line. But I know he can't scold about my language now. Which is why I took the opportunity to say "piss" instead of "pee." It's the small things in life, you know?

"Go, Motti, but be back in five minutes," he says sternly.

I grin. As I start to slide past, he slips a one-lira bill into my hands.

"Come back with a drink," he says with a hint of a smile. "I'm melting,"

I tuck the crumpled bill into my pocket. I'm out of there before he changes his mind. A few people glare at me as I squeeze through the narrow rows of benches.

"Young man, the president of Israel is speaking. Have some respect," an older woman hisses at me. She has a thick Polish accent.

"Excuse me, madam," I say. "I have to use the facilities."

Her face softens for a moment. The older ones are always easy if you stay polite. Plus, I have this face. The Europeans always melt for it. I don't know why. I have pale eyes, freckles, curly brown hair. I recently turned twelve, and with my bar mitzvah less than a year away, I wish I looked less like a cute kid and more like a teenager. No one takes me seriously. The lady reaches for the purse she's holding in her lap. I hear the rustle of cellophane. I quickly slide by before she can offer me a moth-eaten candy. The old ladies all have sticky old lozenges they try to foist on unsuspecting children.

I manage to get away from the rows of benches. There are thousands of people here to see the annual celebration. It rotates every year between Tel Aviv, Haifa, and Jerusalem. It's always a bit tense when it's Jerusalem's turn, since Jordan controls half of it. Israel has West Jerusalem, and Jordan has East Jerusalem with the Old City, the Temple Mount, and the Western Wall. No Jews allowed. Some newspaper editorials argue that we shouldn't have our independence celebration in Jerusalem at all, since it's so close to one of the countries that tried to keep us from being a country. They claim it's confrontational. Other commentators argue that we're allowed to do what we want to do in our half of Jerusalem. The old joke goes that in Israel, if you ask two people what they think, you'll get three opinions.

Usually there's a military parade showing off our tanks, jeeps, and hundreds of marching soldiers with guns. It's great. Last year there were rows and rows of rumbling tanks, everyone cheering and hollering, waving blue and white flags. I yelled so much, I lost my voice for two days. This year, there's hardly anything. It's boring. No tanks. No armored vehicles. Students from Hebrew University have shown up with cardboard cutouts of tanks. They hold them up, as if asking, *Is this the best we can do?*

My dad tells me it's a compromise: we have our celebration in Jerusalem, but we don't aggravate the Jordanians or their lethal army. *I* am aggravated instead.

I've made my way out of the seated crowd. There's a round of applause. The president must have finished his speech. But it's not over. Now Prime Minister Eshkol rises. A pot-bellied man with thick glasses and thinning hair, the prime minister shuffles to the microphone. He rustles the papers of his speech and then begins to speak in his thick Russian accent.

Standing at the rear of the seated crowds, I wave at Gideon up on the stands. For a second, I think he's seen me, but then he turns to look at Eshkol. My brother looks tough and grown-up. I'm used to that, though. Gideon was the captain of our Scout troop when he was in high school. He got the highest grades in his high school class. There's nothing my brother doesn't excel at if he wants to. When he finishes his military service, he plans to study engineering at the Technion, the best science and technology university in Israel.

I look for my dad in the crowd. He's turned in his seat, glaring right at me. I quickly turn and hurry away.

". . . there are no serious threats to our existence in the next decade," Prime Minister Eshkol pronounces. Everyone claps.

I slip away until I can't make out the words, only an amplified murmur. The kiosks with their smell of newsprint, cardamom, and baked bread are all closed for the holiday. But I find a man who's set up a small stand selling soda and candy. I eye the row of candies at the front, but I don't have enough for a soda *and* candy. My father will expect change.

"One Coca-Cola," I say.

Until last year, we couldn't buy Coca-Colas. The League of Arab States threatened to boycott them if they sold any Cokes in Israel. Not just Coca-Cola. There are a whole bunch of products from cars to candy that aren't available in Israel. But Coca-Cola decided last year that they would let Israelis buy their soda. The

Arab League promptly put Coke on their list of boycotted products, forbidding its sale in their countries. So I always make a point to buy some Coke. To make it up to the Coca-Cola company.

The man reaches down and pulls out a cold soda from the cooler at his feet.

"Motti!"

I turn.

"Yossi!"

Yossi is a dark-haired, dark-eyed, wiry kid from my school. We're also in the same Scout troop. He smacks me on the back. I pretend to punch him, and he dodges.

"Get out of here, you hooligans," the man says, waving us away.

We crack up. I throw an arm around Yossi's neck and he rests his arm around my waist. We find a shady spot under a fig tree. I take a big sip. Yossi stares at the Coke.

"Want some?" I hand the glass soda bottle to him.

He drinks deeply, then belches and hands it back.

"Hey," I say indignantly. "You drank half of it!"

He ignores this. "Let's see if there's anyone at the stadium."

The stadium is a scrubby, open field with soccer goals that we made by stacking white rocks in two columns on either side of a rough rectangle. Our soccer stadium.

We head over there. There are three boys kicking a tattered ball. We quickly join in, dribbling and kicking and scoring against each other. It's a hot, sunny day. We pass the soda among the five of us, and the bottle is soon empty, lying on its side by some rocks. My white button-down shirt is streaked with dirt, my nice shoes scuffed. My team is down by two points but I'm not giving up. I have the ball for a throw-in, looking for an open player.

"Motti." A shadow falls over me.

It's Gideon. My older brother has the same light brown curls I do, but his eyes are a deep dark brown, fringed with heavy lashes. Girls always giggle when he passes.

"It's over?" I ask. "Already?"

"It was short." He eyes the empty soda bottle a few feet away. "Dad's looking for you. And he's thirsty."

"*Ach!*" I slap my forehead. "I meant to leave some for him."

Gideon gives me a look.

"See you later," I tell my team and hurl the ball deep toward the opposing team's goal.

Yossi scrambles after it, hollering, "See you tomorrow!"

I follow Gideon down the narrow, cobbled lanes, through our city of high walls and hidden courtyards, passing building after building of pale stone. By law, all buildings in Jerusalem are built out of the same local white rock. It's been this way for three thousand years, since the time of King David.

Gideon's walking fast, and I trot to keep up. We cross through one of the many fields that separate the various neighborhoods. The field is full of knee-high grasses and wildflowers. Off to our right is the grammar school we both attended and where our six-year-old brother, Beni, goes now. I brush too close to a prickly thistle and it scratches my leg, drawing a line of blood.

"Keep up, squirt," Gideon says. Of course, he's not the least bit winded, though we're almost jogging. Gideon has always been very fit and strong. In the first months of his military training, his unit would go on long hikes to "get to know their equipment." These would be 40-kilometer-long daily hikes in full gear. Sometimes Gideon would finish up his hike, then turn around to join the stragglers. He would jog alongside them for the last few kilometers, encouraging them on when they were tired and miserable. They must have found him as annoying as I do.

We're back in our neighborhood now. We skirt around a reeking bag of trash. Two cats slink away as we pass. They're skinny little strays. One of them is all white. I aim a kick as it dashes in front of me, but it twists away and I miss. Stray cats are good at dodging kicks.

A heavy hand falls on my shoulder and Gideon squeezes, his fingers digging painfully into my collarbone. I yelp.

"Don't go out of your way to hurt small creatures," he says, his face right in mine. I knock his hand off me.

"What's it to you?" I demand. I push my face right back in his. My fists bunch at my sides. "They're just stupid stray cats. Everybody kicks them." I wasn't even really thinking about the cat, or wanting to hurt it. It was just in front of me and I kicked.

"'Everyone else does it?'" he mocks. "Is that why you do it? Or because they can't kick you back?"

I hate the rising feeling of shame in my chest. Gideon can always make me feel stupid and incompetent. He can also read me like a book. His face eases as he sees my feelings of guilt. The hand that comes back to rest on my shoulder is soft and warm.

"Motti," he says, "it's too easy to hurt things. You need to have a good reason to hurt something."

"Like what?" I ask, shaking off his hand again.

"If it's going to hurt you first." He pauses.

"Then you strike and strike hard. You knock it into the wall and kill it." I picture it, the cat, neck snapped, falling to the cobbled lane. It turns my stomach. "Otherwise, leave it alone."

We walk the rest of the way home in silence. He ruffles my hair and I dodge, elbowing him in the ribs.

By the time we reach our building, the setting sun casts long shadows over the eucalyptus tree in the front courtyard. The smell of dinner meets us at the door of our apartment.

My mom is a phenomenal cook. Everything that comes out of our cramped kitchen is bound to taste delicious. Schnitzel. Chicken soup. Noodles in butter with parsley. Tomato and cucumber salads. Chocolate cake. Not everyone has such a mother. After a few dinners at my friends' houses and some camping trips with Scouts, I finally realized how lucky I was. This past year, I was constantly hungry and my mother always seemed to have something wonderful coming out of the small oven. Like everyone else, we have to be careful with our money, but there is always enough food to eat.

The table is already set. Beni, my dad, and my mom have clearly been waiting for us. There's chopped salad and olives on the table. A basket with rolls from the bakery. A bowl with hardboiled eggs.

"You found him," my mother exclaims.

"It's not dark yet," I say, defensively.

"But it's Independence Day," my mom scolds. "We are all home. It's a special day."

"The last I saw you, you were going to the bathroom," my father says, shooting me a look from under his lashes. "Must have been one heck of a line."

"I accidentally finished the soda," I say. "I meant to leave you some, but it was hot and . . ."

"Motti got a soda?" Beni cries. "No fair!"

"I found him with that loser friend, Yossi," my older brother reports. "At the field."

"Yossi's not a loser," I say. "His dad was a martyr."

"He's a no-good Moroccan loser," Beni taunts.

I lunge toward my little brother, but Gideon snags me by my upper arm.

"Boys!" my dad barks. "Enough! Beni, you don't speak like that in my house."

Beni glares at me and sticks his tongue out when my dad turns away. My mom, coming in from the kitchen with a pitcher of water, puts a hand on the nape of my neck before I can say something that will get me in more trouble.

"And Motti," my dad says wearily, "we all know you didn't *accidentally* drink an entire bottle of soda."

"No, I just—" I feel my face heat up.

"Come, *motek*," my mom says to me. "Let's have a civilized meal."

I don't argue with my mom. We sit, we eat, and Gideon fills us in on the goings-on with the dignitaries, speakers, and Independence Babies.

"The situation is good," Gideon says. The "situation" is our ongoing balancing act of being a tiny country surrounded by enemies. For the past year and a half there have been more and more raids by terrorists, killing farmers and hitchhikers. We retaliated with our own raids, but they didn't go so well. Soldiers died in those fights, and the attacks keep coming. Still, Gideon says, "Things look stable."

I want to point out that sitting next to the prime minister during a speech doesn't automatically make him some kind of security expert. But for my mom's sake, I don't say it.

"God willing, it will stay that way," my mother says. She knocks on the wooden table three times for good luck.

But it doesn't stay that way—not for long.

Chapter Two
Winds of War

Three days later I come home from school for lunch. Seventh grade starts at seven thirty in the morning, and we are out for the day at one.

After we eat, my parents always lie down for a short rest. Early afternoon is hot and painfully bright. But with the shades drawn and the windows open to catch the smallest breeze, they can usually get their east-facing room comfortable.

Then my dad goes back to work at the woodshop. My mom goes to the market and starts to prepare dinner. Beni goes to the playground to play with his friends. I work on projects for school. When I finish, I head out to catch my friends playing soccer or making mischief.

Today Gideon arrives for lunch, home for a day and a half of leave.

Now that Gideon is in the army, we don't see him often. He volunteered for a combat unit, and he's stationed at a closed base, where secret things happen. Other than the ceremony when he received his Signal Corps insignia, we haven't been allowed on base, though it's only a ten-minute drive away. He usually hitchhikes home every other weekend.

Seeing him in his uniform always amazes me. His beret with the silver Signal Corps pin is tucked under the epaulet of his left shoulder. He looks tough and steady, a real soldier. I have to wait six more years to join the army.

Though he's all smiles as he enters our apartment, he seems unusually distracted as Beni chatters to him about the latest happenings in first grade. Gideon flicks on the radio, even though it's playing a folk music program. I raise an eyebrow at him.

"You're listening to the Gevatron now?" I tease. They're actually a great group, but Gideon has never enjoyed folk music.

He makes a face at the pioneer songs pouring out and switches off the radio.

My mom ladles out apricot chicken, ribbons of steam curling from the sweet and savory meat. My dad passes around a bowl of roasted potatoes, glistening with oil and flecked with salt.

"Yossi says we're going to have another overnight camping trip with Scouts," I say, around a mouthful of delicious chicken. "I told him no way, because our Scout leader said that after last time—"

"Did you hear about Egypt?" Gideon interrupts me.

My parents exchange worried glances.

"We heard. It was on the radio this morning," my dad says.

I stop chewing, distracted from my food. The mood around the table is suddenly serious and grim. Even Beni notices, his eyebrows crinkling as he tries to follow the sudden turn in the conversation.

Egypt, the country at our southern border, is ten times the size of Israel. Their president, Gamal Abdel Nasser, is fond of announcing on

Egyptian state radio that his military will march into Israel on land soaked in our blood. The only country more serious about our annihilation is Syria, at our northern border. Jordan and Lebanon also share a border with us. They don't like us either, but they usually don't go out of their way to dream how great life would be if all the Jews in Israel were dead.

"Nasser says we're planning an attack on Syria and he's going to help them," Gideon says in a low voice.

"We're not attacking Syria," my mom scoffs. "Why would he think that?" It sounds like a rhetorical question, but Gideon sometimes knows more about what's going on because of his work on the base.

"We didn't have tanks in the Independence Day parade," Gideon says. "The Russians are going around telling everyone it's because the tanks are already mobilized on the northern border, preparing to invade Syria."

"But that's a lie!" Beni says. He's little, but he's sharp.

"I knew it," I exclaim. "I said we should have

had tanks in the parade! None of this would be happening if people weren't so worried about offending Jordan."

"We live a kilometer away from the border with Jordan," my dad reminds me. "If there's a war with them, it'll be fought in our neighborhood."

"And Jordan has a treaty with Egypt," added Gideon. "If either one attacks us, so will the other."

Mom sets down her fork as if she's lost her appetite.

"*Is* there going to be a war?" Beni asks in a small voice.

"Sweetheart," my mom says to him, "it'll be fine." She ladles more potatoes onto his plate. "Eat."

"It all comes down to whether the UN troops stay in the Sinai or not," Gideon says. The United Nations has stationed peacekeeping troops in the desert between us and Egypt ever since our last war eleven years ago. They're the main reason more fighting hasn't broken out.

"Those UN troops aren't going anywhere," my dad says. But he sounds worried. He shakes his head "no" when my mom tries to ladle more potatoes onto his plate too. I think she's trying to fill their mouths with food so they stop talking about this.

I notice Beni's eyes, wide and scared.

"No one cares about the stupid UN or Egyptians," I mutter. This talk is ruining our nice meal.

"Motti, be quiet," my dad snaps.

My face turns bright red.

"You'll care if we go to war with them," Gideon adds.

"Calm down," my mom says. "It's not that easy to start a war. God willing, we're a long way from it." She knocks on the table three times and then for good measure says, "*Tfu, tfu, tfu*" against the evil eye. She adds a scoop of potatoes to Gideon's plate. "Now eat."

* * *

After lunch Beni clears the table and I wash the dishes.

"Motti," Beni says, "is it true that Nasser wants to push us into the sea?"

"Maybe it's true," I say. "But the Egyptians already tried that with Moses, and look how that turned out for them. We can take anything they throw at us and still beat them by sundown."

I ruffle his hair, which always annoys him. Plus, my hands are wet and soapy.

Beni makes a disgusted face as he touches his soapy hair. He glares at me. "I'm telling Mom!"

"Dad's going to kill you if you wake them up from their nap again."

Beni narrowed his eyes. But I'm right. He storms off. The front door shuts behind him.

I dry off the last plate and then slip out as well.

As soon as I step out of our apartment building, the sun greets me, bright and warm. Jerusalem sits at the edge of the desert. On one side, there are hills dotted with pine trees, streams, and fertile ground. On the other side, toward Jordan, it's all bare ground, parched and brown. The sun radiates off the desert hills like an oven with the door left open. Bedouins still live on those hills like in ancient times, moving from place to place with their camels and tents.

I've only taken two steps when I see old Mrs. Friedburg making her slow, painful way up the path. She pulls a small metal cart half filled with groceries.

"Motti, open the door for me," she commands in her thick German-accented Hebrew.

Mrs. Friedburg and I have a complicated relationship. On the one hand, she's an evil, grumpy woman who enjoys tattling on the neighborhood kids and getting us into trouble. She's the only adult I know who insists I call her Missus. Everyone else goes by their first name. Even my teachers in school go by the title "morah" or "moreh," meaning teacher, and their first name. On the other hand, Mrs. Friedburg's apartment has a piano.

Before the Second World War, Mrs. Friedburg was a concert piano player and a music teacher in Berlin. When she's in one of her rare good moods, she lets me come into her apartment. She'll play Rachmaninoff and show me basic finger positions and notes. One time she said I had a natural elegance in my wrist positions. I'm not sure what that meant, but it sounded like the nicest thing anyone has ever said to me.

When I look at her piano, the white and black keys stretching out before me in a perfect path, the world just makes sense. Ever since she taught me "Fur Elise," I've played it every time she lets me into her apartment.

But it doesn't happen often. Usually Mrs. Friedburg complains about the heat, the idiots in the government, the dirt, the smell, and how nothing in Israel can compare to the elegant greatness of Germany.

Not surprisingly, most of us native Israeli Sabras don't enjoy hearing how the country that murdered six million Jews is a model of culture and learning. Of course, more than two-thirds of Israel is made up of new immigrants—everyone arriving with their own culture, food, and distinct accents—but they've come here because they consider Israel their home. Mrs. Friedburg never seems to have a kind word about Israel or anyone living in it.

I hold the door open for her as she wheels in her little cart. Her face is wet with sweat.

"*Oy*, this wretched heat," she says, huffing by me.

"Why did you go shopping now? Why not in the morning when it's cool?"

"Cheeky boy!" she harrumphs. "It's none of your business, but I had an appointment in the morning."

"Do you need help with the groceries?" I ask. Mrs. Friedburg lives across the hallway from us. She told me once that she will never move from this apartment because it's too hard to carry the piano down the stairs. Since it's one in the afternoon and all the adults in the building are resting, I also know she won't let me touch her piano. Still, I always try to stay on her good side.

"Bah," she says at my offer. "I know you don't want to spend time with an old woman."

"Okay. *Shalom*, Mrs. Friedburg." I dash off into the bright day before anyone else can stop me.

When I arrive at the field, only Yossi is there.

"Where's everyone else?" I demand. There's usually a good crowd of five or six boys, plenty for a game of soccer.

Yossi shrugs.

"So what do you want to do?" I ask.

"I have a magazine," he says, holding up last week's copy of *Our Country*, the newspaper's weekly edition for children. "Or did you bring marbles?"

I shake my head. I put my hands on my hips, thinking. I can hear the younger kids laughing on the playground near our field. A small band of boys chases another group, probably playing Maccabees and Greeks. The girls are hogging the swings, like they always do.

"Come on," I say, rising to my feet. "Let's go to the fence."

"What? Today?" Yossi is usually game for anything, but going to the fence, the barbed-wire border between Israel and Jordan, is a little dangerous. The Jordanian soldiers generally leave our side of the fence alone, but sometimes people throw rocks. Sometimes there are snipers.

"Yes, of course, today," I say impatiently, the conversation from lunch still on my mind. "Let's see what they're up to."

Our neighborhood is less than a kilometer from the Jordanian border. I head in that direction, knowing that Yossi will follow.

We cut through open fields and narrow streets, racing each other. I'm taller than Yossi but he's faster. He streaks past me, a skinny little blur. We're both wearing leather sandals, and the soles make a smacking noise on the cobbled streets.

We dodge dumpsters overflowing with rotting vegetables, duck under sheets hanging to dry. We're neck and neck, panting and sweating. Apartment buildings go right up to the border. A row of wide cement cones lines Israel's side of the barbed wire fence. A yellow sign says "Border No, Passage" in English, Hebrew, and French. Israeli soldiers keep an eye on the Jordanian side from their post inside a small house.

Jordan is easily visible through the fence. Their soldiers patrol their side. We're not supposed to approach the fence.

We approach the fence.

Every time I come, I count the Jordanian soldiers. I try to remember their faces. You never know what information might be useful. I think of the daring Eli Cohen who spied on the Syrians until he was caught and executed. Or the legendary Yosef Trumpeldor, who died defending Tel-Chai, a Galilee settlement, against Arab raiders in the 1920s. In school, when we study the heroes who helped found Israel, our teachers always remind us how easy we have it compared to what they had to deal with.

If I ever see anything unusual at the fence, I'll tell Gideon and he'll tell his commander. There's one soldier in particular that I see here a lot. He's a little older than most of the usual patrollers, short and slightly fat. Every time he spots me, he winks. One time, he looked over his shoulder and when he saw that no one was looking, he tossed over a small wrapped candy. He had a strong arm and good aim. The candy landed a few feet from me. I scooped it up and examined it closely. The wrapper was covered in Arabic writing. It looked foreign and menacing, but when I unwrapped it, the smell of rose blossoms wafted from it like a dream. I looked up and the soldier grinned at me. I couldn't help smiling back. I wonder if it's okay that I am kind of friendly with a Jordanian.

The Jordanians are led by King Hussein. His grandfather, King Abdullah, was killed seventeen years ago when he came to pray at the Temple Mount in East Jerusalem. An assassin shot him because he was considering peace with Israel. King Hussein was twelve years old at the time, my age, and standing at his grandfather's side when the king was shot.

My soldier is not at the fence today.

A different soldier sees us. He hitches his rifle, then slings it off his shoulder. Yossi squeaks in fear.

"Let's get out of here!"

My friend turns and runs. I wait a beat, glaring at the soldier. We lock eyes. My heart thumps in my chest. My brain is telling me: *Go, run away.* The soldier's face is flat, blank, but his eyes glint darkly. He holds his rifle in both hands, staring me down. My legs ignore my mind. My fists clench by my sides.

On the other side of that fence is the rest of Jerusalem, the heart and soul of my people.

The Old City. King David's tower. The Mount of Olives. And most importantly, the Western Wall. It's part of the retaining wall from the Temple, destroyed first by the Babylonians and a second, final time by the Romans two thousand years ago. It is the holiest and most important place for all Jews. We pray in synagogue facing east, the direction of the Western Wall. We end every Passover meal with the pledge "Next year in Jerusalem!" We don't mean West Jerusalem. We mean the Western Wall.

Jordan controls it. And they won't let us Jews near it. When we lost the Old City in the War of Independence, all the Jews fled into West Jerusalem, and no one's been allowed back to the Old City since.

So I stand there and glare at the soldier. He stares flatly back at me. He spits to the side, then lifts his rifle, taking aim at me. My heart races so fast, it feels like it will explode in my chest, saving the soldier a bullet. *Run, run,* my mind screams. But my knees are locked. I can't move. I watch the soldier as if in slow motion. The barrel slowly lifts, the empty black hole coming up.

Suddenly, someone grabs my arm and yanks me hard. I spin, breaking eye contact with the soldier. Yossi has me. He tugs hard, pulling me off balance. I trip and stumble to keep to my feet. He pants, "Move, Motti, *move*!"

My knees unlock. My feet finally listen to my screaming mind. We fly out of there.

Chapter Three
Post Office War Cabinet

"Did you hear the latest joke about the prime minister?" the man in line at the post office asks my dad. "He's at a café and the waitress asks, 'Tea or coffee?' Eshkol thinks and thinks. Finally he holds out his cup and says, 'Some of each.'"

"Please, that's an old one." It's a long line, and the post office is hot and stuffy.

"Okay, so how about this? Eshkol says to a crowd of American businessmen, 'Want to know how to make a small fortune in Israel? Start with a big one.'"

"Ha, ha. I've heard that one too." The jokes are getting less funny. Everyone was already unhappy with our unpopular, hesitant prime minister. His recent uninspiring speech on the radio hasn't helped. The Egyptian army is at our border and Nasser, their charismatic president, has demanded that the UN peacekeeping force on the border leave. Stationed between Israel and Egypt, those peacekeepers are literally keeping peace. No UN, no peace. There's a feeling of tension and fear in the air. Everyone's preoccupied with news, never missing the hourly update while our government leaders argue and hesitate.

Gideon has not been home in days. His leave was cancelled and he had to return to the base early. I've heard my parents talking. Their low, worried voices keep me awake late into the night.

"Abba, are we going to war?" I ask. I try to sound brave and unconcerned, not like Beni the other day.

"No," my dad says. "As long as the UN forces stay put, there's nothing to worry about."

"Didn't you hear?" the man in front of us says. He has thin white hair that floats around his head like a dandelion puff. I can't help noticing the blue-green tattooed scrawl of numbers on his arm. He's a concentration camp survivor.

"What?" asks my dad.

"They just announced it on the radio. All UN forces are leaving Egypt." He has a sharp Hungarian accent.

I look at my dad.

"Abba, now are we going to war?"

He presses his lips together until his mouth turns into a thin white line.

"We're still a long way from war."

"Not that long, my friend," the Hungarian says in a mocking voice. "Mark my words: the UN pulls out, the Egyptian tanks start rolling across the Negev into Israel."

"No, no," says the woman behind us. She's wearing a purple housedress and thick-soled shoes. "The Americans will put a stop to that." From her accent I can tell she's a Sabra like us, a native-born Israeli.

"Wishful thinking," says the Hungarian in front of us. "No one is coming to help us."

"You're wrong!" says a thin man in a white button-down shirt and black trousers, an Iraqi

Jew. "The Russians are behind this business with Egypt, so the Americans will back us, even if it's just to cause trouble for the Russians."

"Mark my words: we're going to be on our own," says the know-it-all Hungarian. "We were on our own in Europe during the Holocaust, on our own here in 1948, and we're on our own now. The Jews have no friends."

"How can you talk like that?" scoffs the woman behind my dad.

The arguments continue as we scoot forward in line. Finally, it's our turn. We buy a sheet of stamps and a package of aerograms. This stationery for overseas letters folds into thirds and the little flaps seal it into a self-contained envelope. My mom's sister, Aunt Rachel, works in the Israeli embassy in Washington, D.C. My mom writes to her every week.

My dad and I stop by the bakery on our way home. There is bread and several kinds of baked goods on the shelves: savory onion rolls, cheese-filled *borekas*, dry crumbly cookies, and yeasty chocolate rolls. My dad buys a loaf of bread and a large triangular *boreka*. He tucks the bread, wrapped in thin white paper, under his arm and hands me the paper bag with the savory pastry. I tear into it as we walk. Buttery crumbs and sesame seeds scatter at my feet. I hand him the other half and he bites into it, finishing it in two big gulps.

I usually run these errands for my mom by myself or with Beni, but my dad woke up from his nap early today and offered to join me.

"*Nu*, Motti," my dad says. "You going to tell me what's going on with you?"

"What?"

"Yossi's mother told us you went to the fence at the border. That you taunted the soldiers there. Is that true?"

"She's exaggerating." I kick a small pebble on the sidewalk and watch it ping away.

"Did you go to the fence?"

"Yossi is a tattletale," I say hotly. "What's he doing running to his mom and telling her this stuff about me?"

My dad pins me with one of his looks. "Yes or no?"

"Yes." I look away.

My dad rubs a hand across his face. He has the strongest hands of anyone I've ever met—what my grandmother always calls "good hands." He just seems to know how to make things work, to fix things. That's probably why he's a carpenter. But today everything about him seems less certain, less steady. He looks tired.

"Motti, you have a daredevil heart. But you also have a bright mind. You need to use that mind. This is not the time to play games with Jordanian soldiers. I don't know where the situation is going." There are beads of sweat on his upper lip, and a trickle of moisture runs down the side of his face. "You heard that amateur war cabinet at the post office. Right now, everything is tense."

"Yeah, Abba, sure. I hear you. But it wasn't that bad. Yossi's mom really exaggerated."

"I haven't seen the situation this tense since '56," he says tightly. There was a war with Egypt in 1956, when I was one. "It's not like when I was a kid," he continues.

My dad used to live in the Jewish Quarter in the Old City. The Jews and Arabs in the

Old City got along pretty well in those days. I've grown up hearing stories of my dad's good friend Daoud, a Jordanian guy. Back when they were kids, Daoud loved tinkering with model planes. Every time my dad went to his house, Daoud's mother would feed them delicious treats that looked like little bird nests, with pistachios for eggs, dripping with honey. But they haven't seen each other since the Independence War in 1948, when they were young men.

"Don't go looking for trouble," my dad says. "Trouble finds you easy enough without your help." He puts a hand on my shoulder. We come to a stop in the middle of the bustling sidewalk. "Motti, don't try to be a hero."

But that's exactly what I want to be. I stiffen and shake his hand off me.

"Heroes die young," he says. "Serve your country—not to mention your family—by living a good long life."

I shove my hands in my pockets, scowling at the sidewalk. I bet Eli Cohen's family didn't tell him that. They let him spy in Syria and have thrilling adventures saving our country.

My dad sighs. "All right, let me put it another way. There are all kinds of heroes."

We cross the road, hurrying to get to the other side as a blue-and-cream colored Egged bus lumbers down the street. It belches a thick cloud of exhaust on its way past us.

"A hero is someone who can rise above his fears and his problems, and help others. It's *not* heroic to throw your life away. That's a disgrace."

"Okay, but—"

"In fact, we have a hero in our building."

"We do?" I know everyone in our building. I can't imagine who he means. I try to picture our ancient upstairs neighbor Shlomo charging a sand dune in the First World War.

"Mrs. Friedburg," my dad says.

"What?" I almost choke.

"Oh, yes," my dad says, in all seriousness. "She's a tremendously brave and strong person."

"First: she's tiny, not strong," I say, ticking my points off on my fingers. "Second: she's mean!"

"Think, Motti! Think about what she's been through," my dad says, a little impatiently. "She lost everything: her country, her home, her family, her language, her profession. And still, she perseveres. It was devastating for my parents to flee from the Old City into West Jerusalem, but at least for them the language and culture was the same here. Mrs. Freidburg immigrated to a new land. She learned a new language. She made a new home after she lost every single member of her family. There aren't a lot of people who would be able to do that. She's a hero because she lives on."

That doesn't sound like a real hero to me.

"Do you understand?" my dad asks.

I just shrug. I know my dad is smart, but sometimes he has weird ideas. Spies are heroes. Paratroopers are heroes. Little old ladies who complain about the heat are not heroes.

My dad sighs. I can feel him looking at me in frustration. He pulls out a folded handkerchief from his pocket and mops the sweat on his face.

"Do you think Saba and Safta can come for Shabbat dinner this week?" I ask to change the subject.

"Good idea, let's ask them," my dad says. He ruffles my hair, and I know he isn't mad anymore. But from the way his shoulders stay high and stiff, I can tell he's still worried about *the situation.*

We walk on, no longer talking.

Chapter Four
No More Teachers

That night we finish dinner quickly. No one lingers at the table with the mood so tense. With the UN troops gone, the radio news announced, Egyptian troops have started moving into the region.

"As long as Egypt doesn't close the Straits of Tiran, they can mobilize their troops all they want," my dad says. He's in his usual seat, an orange upholstered chair near the living room window. He takes a deep puff from his cigarette.

My dad quit smoking six months ago.

"But if they close the water to Israeli ships, then we have a serious problem," he adds.

He's talking about the finger of water from the Red Sea that reaches between Saudi Arabia and Egypt to Eilat, Israel's southernmost city. It connects Israel to ships sailing from Africa. Eilat, on the shore of the Red Sea, is a popular vacation spot. Not that I've ever been there. The only holiday I've had was when my dad and I went to Tel Aviv to visit my cousin. But I've been learning a lot of geography at school lately, as my teacher, Moreh Dudi, uses current events in our lessons.

"They'd be crazy to do that," my mom says. She runs a hand through her short dark hair. She sits on the couch, one leg jiggling with tense energy. "You can't tell a country it can't send ships to its own port. That's an act of war."

"The Arabs have been looking for a way to destroy us for nineteen years." My dad grinds out his half-smoked cigarette into a small saucer he's using as an ashtray. "Hate can make people unpredictable."

My mom clears her throat loudly. Beni's walked into the room and is listening.

They end their discussion, looking strained. I catch them looking at the framed photo of Gideon in his olive-green army uniform. The picture was taken at the end of his paratrooper course. He stands tall and proud, getting his insignia pinned on.

No one has to say it. If there's war, my brother will be fighting in it.

That night I lie in bed, Beni's soft breaths filling the room. I hear the low murmurs of my parents talking late into the night. Their stress seems to fill the apartment until I can feel it pressing down on me.

* * *

The next day at school, Moreh Dudi doesn't arrive. We sit around waiting for him. Pretty soon, someone shoots a spitball, and the next thing you know, the whole class erupts. Spitballs are flying, chairs tumble over as the boys dodge, the girls shriek and smack at our heads.

"Class!" screams Morah Pnina, the other seventh-grade teacher. "Enough!"

We stop, turning to look at her with blinking, innocent eyes.

Her hands on her hips, she takes a deep, aggravated breath. She's a tall lady and tough, not someone to mess with.

"Moreh Dudi has been called up to active duty. Gather your things. You are coming to my class. I will teach both seventh-grade classes until he returns."

I exchange goggle eyes with Yossi. There are forty kids in each class.

Someone raises a hand.

"Excuse me, Morah Pnina, how are we going to fit? There aren't enough chairs in your class for all of us."

"You'll make do," she says, sternly. "Sit on the floor and be grateful for your education."

I grab my school bag. Yossi does the same. Morah Pnina nods approvingly at us.

"Kids, we all have to adjust," she says, more kindly. "We need to be strong and smart, and pray that everything will work out okay."

So we all press into the next-door classroom. It's hot and stuffy. It's hard to hear Morah Pnina over the rustling and shuffling of eighty kids. But we take notes, balancing our papers on top of books on our knees. Some kids share chairs, perching half a butt cheek on their side of the chair, bumping elbows as they write.

"How long will Moreh Dudi be in the army?" someone asks.

Morah Pnina is silent. Her face is pinched. She looks tired.

"As long as he needs to be," she says, unwilling to be drawn into a conversation about it.

I wonder if she'll dismiss us early, but she's even tougher than I gave her credit for. She keeps us until the last minute before the bell rings.

"Tomorrow, everyone come straight to my room. We are not going to let a small matter of politics get in the way of algebra!"

When I go home for lunch, I find out that my teacher wasn't the only one called up from the reserves.

My mom has set the table, and there are only three plates out.

"Where's Abba?" I ask.

"He's been called up," my mom says. "The

radio announced his unit's code." She's trying to sound matter-of-fact, but I can hear the worry in her voice. It's called a silent mobilization. My father has told me about it. Each unit has a unique call name like "golden apples" or "singing nightingale," something random and obscure. If, in the course of a news update, the announcer happens to mention the unit's call name, it means they need to report to their commander immediately. To make sure no one misses the announcement, everyone who hears it is assigned three or four people to personally tell. My dad's people are all in our neighborhood. All he needed to do was walk a few buildings over, knock on some doors, and then pack his bags and head out.

If his unit has been called up, that means we're one step closer to war.

"Egypt has moved cannons to the Strait of Tiran," my mom explains. "No Israeli ships are allowed past."

I'm still mulling over what this means for Israel and what we're going to do next when Beni arrives from school, full of news.

"Our principal wasn't there today!" he cries. "He's been called up."

"So has Abba," I say.

"Oh." Beni wraps his arms around his middle. "Did the war start?" he asks quietly.

"*Tfu, tfu, tfu,*" my mom says against the evil eye. "Nothing so bad as that."

It's a strange meal with just the three of us. The small clinks of the forks and knives on the ceramic plates sound like thunder. My mother chews and chews, but hardly eats any of the food on her plate.

"I'm going out," I announce, pushing back my plate.

"Be back before dark," my mother says sharply.

"I know," I say.

"Can I come with you?" Beni asks.

"No."

"Pleeeease!"

"No!"

"And for the love of God," my mom says, her voice low and deadly serious, "stay away from the border."

I race over to Yossi's house through the narrow streets that separate our apartments. It's quieter than usual. Hardly any buses running and no students milling at the bus stops. A skinny white cat dashes in front of me. I almost trip.

"Stupid cat," I mutter. I'm about to kick it, but I stop, remembering Gideon's words.

As if it can read my mind, the cat stops running and turns to look at me. It has clear green eyes. One of its ears has a notch in it, as if it had been ripped or bitten.

"Scat!" I hiss. "Go away."

It doesn't move.

"Gideon isn't always right," I tell the cat. "I might still kick you."

It lifts a paw and licks it, as if daring me to come at it. I have to laugh.

"You've got chutzpah, Cat—I'll give you that." It flicks its notched ear as if it's winking at me. There's a clang from across the street. We both turn to look at the sound. When I look back toward the cat, he's gone.

I walk the rest of the way to Yossi's apartment, feeling green eyes at my back.

Yossi's mom opens the door, looking resigned to see me.

"Motti," she says.

"*Shalom,*" I say. "Can Yossi come out?"

Yossi is an only child. His dad was a taxi driver. When Yossi was a baby, his dad drove someone who asked to be taken to an Arab village. When Yossi's dad got there, men were waiting for him. It took police three days to find his body. They never found the murderers.

Yossi's mom is very protective of Yossi. And ever since Yossi and I got into trouble for throwing grapes off the roof of their apartment building two years ago, she hasn't liked me. She thinks I'm a bad influence on him.

"Yossi can't go out today," she says in a flat voice.

"Why?"

I see Yossi pop his head out from the around the corner. He looks miserable.

"I know what you did the other day," she says, leaning close into my face. "War is coming. You can't do stupid things like that now. One of you will get shot. And I won't let it be Yossi!"

She hisses the words, and I flinch as some spit hits my face. She braces her arm across the doorjamb, as if to stop me from physically crossing the threshold into their apartment. Her nails are bitten down to the quick.

"It wasn't that bad," I say, my shoulders hunched around my ears.

"The Arabs are saying that the streets will run with Jewish blood. That's not bad? Syria is mobilizing to the north, Egypt to the south. Jordan is a kilometer to the east. We're surrounded." She takes a ragged breath. "The history books will say the Jews held onto their country for nineteen years before they were scattered to the winds again."

Goosebumps race across my skin at her words. It can't be that bad. It can't.

I lift my chin. "We'll fight them back."

"Motti, if we mobilize all our soldiers, we have less than a hundred thousand. Egypt alone has more than twice that. With the other Arab armies, they have half a million soldiers. They have five times as many tanks and planes as Israel. And we can't keep our soldiers mobilized.

How was school without your teacher today?" she asks sarcastically. I don't say a thing, my face a frozen mask. "Who's going to drive the buses? Who's going to work in the shops? We can't keep it up."

"We'll do whatever we have to do," I insist.

She shakes her head. "Syria sits on top of the Kinneret, our main water source. All they have to do is take control of it and wait for us to collapse. And then they will come in and slaughter us."

"That's not true!"

"It *is* true," she says with finality. The door closes in my face.

Chapter Five
Pit Stop

We can hear the shrill ring of a telephone coming from the upstairs neighbors. The Geffens are the only ones in our six-unit building who have a phone. There's silence as they answer the call. Two minutes later, there's a desperate knocking at our door.

I open it to see Shira Geffen, the eleven-year-old from upstairs.

"Your dad's on the phone," she says with breathless excitement. "He wants to talk to your mom."

My dad is stationed with the central command, less than half a mile from our house. My mom drops the pants she's hemming and dashes upstairs in her slippers.

The Geffens don't mind when people call their phone to talk to someone in our building. For one thing, it means they always know the latest gossip. They were the first to find out when my aunt Rachel had her baby and the first to know that Shlomo's sister had passed away.

Shira Geffen and I are in the same Scout troop. She's skinny and tanned, with dark, curly hair that reaches the middle of her back when it's not braided. Shira's family is more observant than we are, so her mom always wears a scarf to cover her hair, and they keep strict Shabbat, not turning on lights or cooking on the Sabbath. We're a little more flexible. My parents have been known to turn on a lamp and make coffee. Even though the Geffens don't use electricity on the Sabbath, they love it the rest of the week. Shira told me that her family might get a television in their apartment. If they do, Shira promised I could come watch the shows.

My parents talk on the phone for a few minutes, and then my mom comes downstairs looking relieved. It's the first time she's talked to him since he was deployed. Though he spent the past few days on base, he told her he thinks he'll be able to come home soon.

"His biggest complaint is the helmets," she tells Shira, Beni, and me. "They've run out of the regular issue, so he got a British steel helmet from the First World War." She snorts a little sadly. "Waste not, want not."

"My dad got the same kind of helmet," Shira says. "He says it looks like he's wearing a frying pan." Our fathers have been with the same unit for nineteen years. Ever since they finished with regular military service, they've been part of a reserve unit that serves one month every year. Soldiers stay with the same unit for the rest of their military service until discharge in their late forties. Our dads are in a quartermaster unit, which means they're in charge of supplies.

Shira leaves to go back upstairs. We can hear her baby brother crying. Shira's mom, Ofra, is nice enough, but she's strict and yells at us boys if we're noisy. The baby, Yoram, is a poor sleeper. If a rowdy kid accidentally wakes up the baby, you better believe our parents end up getting an earful over it.

My mom folds the pants she's working on and sets them aside. Then she notices the book lying on the end table by the couch.

"Oh, Gideon forgot his book," my mom says. "What a pity."

Gideon always likes to have a book with him. Unlike some soldiers who read westerns or sexy novels, Gideon never wants to waste his time. He says he wants to fill his mind with the best. A few years ago, my parents bought a set of pocket-sized editions of the greatest texts in Western literature translated into Hebrew. My brother is slowly making his way through the entire collection.

"I'll bring it to him," I volunteer.

"I'll come too," Beni chirps.

We'll take any excuse to go see Gideon at the base. We're not allowed inside, of course. But it's exciting to go to the gate guard and tell him we're Gideon's brothers. The guard radios someone on the base, and a few minutes later Gideon comes jogging over. It's one thing to see him in his uniform at home, but it's another to see him on the base. Jeeps drive around. There are heavy guns and a general air of toughness and efficiency. I can't wait until I'm eighteen.

I glance at the book my mom has handed me, *All Quiet on the Western Front*. It has a sketch of a sad-looking soldier on the cover. I skim the summary on the back. It's a war novel, which I like. Maybe I'll read it after Gideon finishes it.

"They might not be able to get it to him," my mom warns us. "I'm sure they're extremely busy."

"I know," I say. "Worst case, we'll leave it with the guard at the gate."

My mom kisses the top of my head.

"You're a sweet boy," she says.

Though the bus for our route should come every ten minutes, Beni and I wait nearly an hour. Many of the buses have been lent to the military to move troops. With almost all the drivers now called up to active duty, Egged, the national bus service, has pulled former drivers out of retirement. We board the blue-and-cream colored bus and I pay the driver, who is white-haired and wrinkled. His khaki Egged uniform hangs loosely on his frame. Beni and I find a seat together.

The radio plays "Listener Favorites," and listeners call in with requests. I nod my head to the beat. First Elvis. Then the Beatles. Beni and I share a grin. We love the Beatles. And then the new hit song, "Jerusalem of Gold," comes on. The normal chatter stops. Naomi Shemer, a popular Israeli composer, wrote this love song to our divided city, a city of "gold and bronze and light."

Though the song has only been out a couple of weeks, everyone knows the words. Before long, the whole bus sings together. As if it's a song we all knew somewhere in our hearts but had forgotten until Naomi Shemer set it free.

Of course, Jerusalem is not a golden city at all. It's white and gray and dirty. But the song fills us with hope and longing for the city that we dream of, a city filled with light, our spiritual home.

The song ends, and there's a loud beep from the radio announcing a news break. Everyone on the bus grows quiet. The same sharp expression of worry makes the people around us look almost alike.

This just in: Charles de Gaulle, the president of France, says that his country will not give aid to Israel in the case of hostilities. Though France signed a commitment to Israel's security, de Gaulle announces, "That was 1957. This is 1967."

The woman behind me gasps in horror. I think of the Holocaust survivor from the post office who predicted this: *The Jews have no friends.*

Beni and I exchange glances.

As soon as the announcer ends his news update, riders start debating the meaning of this.

"We never should have sent Abba Eban, he can't negotiate worth a damn!"

"Without France behind us, England won't back us either. Those Europeans stick together, just you watch."

"War is coming. There's going to be war, and we're going to fight alone. No one is coming to our rescue."

I can barely hear the next song over the shrill predictions.

Beni's eyes grow wider and wider. Luckily, our stop is next. My brother and I hurry off.

"My stomach hurts," he says, grabbing his belly and looking miserable.

"Don't let those guys scare you," I say. "People like that are always too dramatic."

"No, I really have to go!"

"What, they scared the poop out of you?"

"No!" he says. "But I can't help it."

"You have to hold it!" I scold. "There's no place to go."

But I can tell he really does need to go. Beni always feels stress in his stomach. I look around—there's not much cover. A long stretch of road, a bus-stop sign with a bench, and the barbed-wire fence running along the perimeter of the base.

"Motti, this is an emergency," he says desperately.

Taking a leak against a tree is one thing. Dropping your pants and taking a dump in plain view is harder to do. Plus we don't have any paper to wipe with.

"We're going to have to ask to go on the base," I say. "There's no other place to go."

Beni's brown eyes are wide and worried.

We walk along the barbed wire fence until we reach the front gate. The dirt is parched under our feet, and little puffs of dust rise behind us as we walk. A soldier immediately comes out to meet us.

"We're Gideon Laor's brothers," I say. "He left his book at home."

Beni elbows me, giving me an urgent look.

"And my little brother really needs to use the facilities," I say in my most polite voice.

"No civilians allowed," the soldier says in a bored tone. His hair is shaggy and his uniform is wrinkled and slouchy.

"Please," I say, "it's an emergency."

"I'm sorry. I can't let you boys in."

Beni moans. He reaches back and clutches his behind, as if he could physically stop the poop from coming out. The soldier's eyes grow wide as the severity of the situation becomes clear to him.

"You're going to have a mess here," I warn. "He's only six, he can't hold it much longer."

"Who's your older brother again?" the guard asks.

"Gideon Laor," I say.

"I think I know Gideon," he says, a bit uncertainly. "Wait here." He goes inside the little guard shack and grabs the handheld radio. He talks into it, listens to the garbled reply. He looks at us with narrowed eyes. Beni hops a little in anxious anticipation.

"I really need to go!" he calls out.

"It's okay," I tell my brother. "He'll let us in. If not," I raise my voice, "we'll find a tree or something." I know the soldier heard me because he makes a face. He talks a little more animatedly into the radio. Beni and I exchange hopeful looks.

The guard comes out again. "Your brother's on his way. He'll take you to the bathroom. But as soon as you flush, you have to come right back out." He leans close, putting his face right in front of ours. "You're really not allowed inside. We're doing this as a special favor. You understand?"

Beni and I both nod vigorously. This is amazing! I want to kiss Beni. I wish I had thought of this strategy before. We're going onto Gideon's base! I do my best to keep a grin of excitement off my face, but something must show because the soldier gives a small smile. He understands.

A minute later, Gideon comes jogging up. I worry that he'll be angry, but he's smiling.

"Hey, you rascals," he says.

"I hear there's a big emergency."

"I have to go, Gideon! I feel it coming out!"

"No time to waste, then." He places a hand on Beni's shoulder, and I walk on his other side. I stand a little taller and try to look like I belong.

The base is hopping. Soldiers in uniform hurry from place to place. The buildings are made of corrugated metal walls and have low, curved roofs. Sand-colored jeeps are parked in neat rows. I try to remember everything. As soon as I turn eighteen, I'm going to volunteer for a combat unit—maybe paratroopers, the elite fighters who are the first to rush into battle. A unit in tight formation jogs by us, shouting out refrains to the beat of their boot falls.

"The mess hall's over there," Gideon says, pointing at one building. "Barracks over there," he points over to another building.

"Bathroom!" Beni reminds him.

"Over here." We enter a small building and walk down a narrow corridor. It smells like machine oil, sweat, and coffee. There are lots of doors on either side. We pass a door that's open, and I peek in. Rows of desks with soldiers poring over reports and maps. I try to see what they're looking at, but Gideon pulls me forward.

"Here, Beni," he says and opens the door to the men's room. The smell of urine hits us. Beni makes a face. "Get used to it, kid," Gideon says with a grin. "One day you'll just be happy that there's an actual latrine to use and not a hole in the ground." He pushes Beni in and closes the door after him. The two of us stand outside the door.

"You're something else, Motti," my brother says, ruffling my hair. "Did you put Beni up to this?"

"No!" I say indignantly. "I was taking care of him! He would have crapped his pants if I didn't convince the guard to let us in."

"Watch the language," Gideon says, smacking the back of my head. "You're not in the army yet."

A female soldier hurries by, carrying a tall stack of folders. She does a double take when she sees me.

"The recruits get younger and younger," she says.

Gideon grins back, his annoyance with me instantly gone. "Dorit, this is my brother, Motti."

"Nice to meet you," I say. It has not escaped me that Dorit is beautiful, with striking green eyes and a heart-shaped face. Of course she knows Gideon. She can't take her eyes off my brother.

"I see the resemblance," she says, with a flirting look. "Handsome men must run in the family."

The tops of my cheeks turn hot and red.

"Motti is much better looking," Gideon says easily. "And wait until you see my youngest brother. Beni is going to be a real heartbreaker."

That's the thing about my brother. He might pound me or tease me when it's just the family, but if there's anyone else around, he only heaps praise.

"There's another Laor boy?" Dorit asks.

"We're the Three Musketeers," Gideon says, putting his arm around me. "My brothers are the best." Gideon is a head taller than me. My mom keeps promising I'll hit a growth spurt, but at this moment, I'm glad at how well I fit under my brother's arm. I lean my head against his warm, strong chest. His voice rumbles in my ear.

"I can see that," Dorit says with a real smile. "But Captain Levy is looking for you. You guys have your chem drill."

Gideon straightens with a jolt.

"Can you keep an eye on Motti for five minutes?" he asks. "I got to run."

Dorit hesitates, the happy look on her face freezing.

"They're leaving as soon as my little brother finishes in there. I'd walk them out, but I can't stay." He flashes a crooked grin at her. "Be a pal."

She sighs and gives him a rueful smile.

"You're the best," he tells Dorit, giving her a quick friendly pat on the shoulder before she can change her mind.

Gideon gives me a brief, hard hug. I take a

deep breath of his smell: starchy uniform, soap, metal, and sweat.

"Be good," he tells me quietly. Then he takes off, hurrying to join his unit. In fact, everyone on base seems to be in a hurry. There's a buzzing energy in the air.

Without Gideon here, Dorit and I look at each other with nothing to say. Dorit shifts impatiently, transferring the stack of files she's holding from one arm to the other.

"So, you're ten years old?" she asks, trying to make small talk.

"I'm twelve!" I say, insulted.

"Oh. Sorry."

We stand silently for a couple of achingly slow, awkward minutes.

"Do you need to go check on your little brother?" she suggests testily.

"He knows what to do in there," I say.

There're no sounds coming from the bathroom. No toilet flushing or faucet running. Dorit taps her foot nervously. Her boots are meticulously shiny. I have to resist the urge to scuff one with my sandal.

"You sure he's okay in there?" she asks.

"Yes. He always takes a long time."

She glances at her watch.

"Motti, listen, I can't wait much longer. The colonel is waiting for these files. This is really not a good time."

"You can go," I say. "I'll wait here for Beni and then we'll leave straight away."

She hesitates.

"It's okay," I say. I give her my most charming and trustworthy smile. "I know the way out."

She looks at her watch again, then scans the hallway, but there's no one else around for her to foist us onto. All the doors are closed. There's no one but us in the corridor.

"Really," I say. "We're fine here. Sometimes he sits on the toilet for half an hour."

Her eyes widen in horror.

"As soon as he's out, you have to leave," she says in a low voice. "Do you understand? This is a closed base, and you know the situation we're under."

I nod solemnly.

"We cannot afford distractions. Everyone is very busy; the base is on high alert."

"As soon as Beni's out, we'll go," I promise her. "We were never planning to come in at all. It was an emergency." I put on my best serious and dependable look. "He's only six."

"Okay. I'm trusting you," she says.

I nod again, and she buys it. Adjusting her grip on the files, she hurries down the hall.

Three minutes later, I hear the toilet flush and the pipes clanging as Beni washes hands. He comes out, drying his hands on his shorts. He freezes when he sees there's only me waiting for him.

"Where's Gideon?" he asks.

"He had to go," I say, a smile slowly spreading across my face. "But we can stay."

Chapter Six

No Sense of Direction

Beni and I walk out of the building. I've always wanted to know what goes on at a military base, and this is the best chance I'm ever going to get.

I stand outside the heavy metal door, breathing in the atmosphere. There's a slight tang of something burning. I can hear distant rifle shots. Gideon told me there's a firing range on the base. Some of the units must be practicing. The base feels swollen, like there are too many people for the space. But there's a sense of intense focus, not as much worry and panic as on the bus ride.

"I thought we were supposed to leave," Beni says when he sees I'm in no hurry to return to the gate.

"Oh, yes, we are. But . . ." I slide a glance over at him. "What can we do? We have a bad sense of direction." I shake my head slowly. "A *very* bad sense of direction."

Beni's mouth forms a perfect "O" of understanding. A slow smile spreads across his impish face.

"Where to first?" he asks. I grin at my brilliant little brother.

It's a large base, black tarmac spreading out in all directions. There's a large silver hangar with massive doors rolled shut.

"There," I say, pointing toward the hangar. "Let's go see what's in there."

The number-one rule for sneaking is not to scurry. Don't look over your shoulder. Don't act sneaky. Of course, it's hard to "blend in" on base since we're the only ones not in uniform, and also a foot shorter than everyone else. So I basically need us to be invisible. Which means we can't stand exposed on the tarmac. We hug the building, staying close to its metallic walls. I'm counting on the fact that everyone is too caught up in their own mission to really pay attention.

My plan is to leapfrog from building to building until we can get to the hangar and peek inside those giant metal doors.

But I underestimate the army.

We're only at the second building on the way to the hangar when someone shouts, "Hey! What are you doing here?"

"Don't turn around," I whisper to Beni. "Just keep going."

"Stop!" the man yells.

Beni's eyes bug out of his head, and his grip crushes my hand. The other hand goes to his stomach, as if it's cramping.

"Relax!" I hiss at him.

I casually look over my shoulder to see who's shouting. A sergeant glares at us from the doorway of an adjacent building. I wave happily. His expression wavers.

There's a building in front of us. Without hesitating, I open the door and pull Beni in behind me.

"What are we doing here?" he whispers. "What is this place?"

"I don't know, doesn't matter. We had to get

out of sight. Come on!" I tug Beni behind me, pulling us deeper down the hallway. I try every door along the way, but they're all locked. The main building door swings open, and the sergeant comes in after us.

The next door I try opens.

"Here!" I hiss to Beni and pull him inside.

There are five or six people in the room huddled over two military radios, chain smoking. A gray cloud fills the top third of the room. The military radios crackle gibberish, each garbled transmission ending with "Over." A civilian radio in the corner is tuned to GALATZ, the military public-radio station. It plays patriotic songs at low volume.

I can't tell if the soldiers crouching over the radios really understand what the incoming messages say, but they exchange looks every so often and jot something down on spiral pads.

Suddenly, someone grabs Beni and me by the upper arms and yanks us out of the radio room.

The sergeant shakes me hard enough to make my head snap. My teeth catch and clink together.

"Leave him alone!" Beni shouts. "Let him

go!" He rams himself against the large man. The soldier, now enraged, lets go of me with one hand and grabs Beni, wrenching him like a rag doll by the arm.

"Don't touch my brother!" I scream and kick the man in the knee. He grunts but doesn't let go.

"What the hell is going on here?" A major steps out of one of the locked rooms. He's completely bald and has the wide, stocky build of a wrestler.

"Sir," the sergeant says breathlessly, "I found these kids wandering around the base. I just pulled them out of the communication room."

The major's eyes narrow.

"Who are you?" he asks sharply. "Who let you in here?"

Beni starts to say something, but I quickly jump in. I don't want him to mention Gideon's name—it might get him into trouble.

"My brother needed to use the bathroom," I say earnestly. "We didn't touch anything."

"What the hell?" the major says. "What do you think this is? Grand Central bus station? A tourist attraction? This is a closed base!"

By now several more doors have opened, people stepping out into the hallway to see what the commotion is about.

I hear a choked squeak of horror. "Motti, Beni! What are you still doing here?"

The major turns to see Dorit standing by one of the doors, looking appalled.

"Corporal, you know these boys?" he demands. His shiny scalp has grown flushed with sweat and frustration.

"Yes," she says faintly. The major gives her a murderous look. "I didn't let them in!" she protests. "I saw them earlier today. There was, ah . . . ah . . . a medical emergency." She glares at me and Beni. "I think they're feeling better now. They must have gotten lost on their way to the gate. Right?"

I am so grateful she doesn't rat out Gideon.

"Yes," I say. "We have a bad sense of direction!"

"For God's sake," the major says in exasperation. "I don't have time for this. Get them out. Now!"

The sergeant lets us go and tugs at his uniform, straightening it with a yank. The tops of his ears are bright red. His eyes are narrowed in anger. He drops his steak-sized hand on the back of my neck, pulling me toward the door at the end of the hallway.

"I'll walk them out," Dorit says, to my great relief. The sergeant's meaty hand tightens on the back of my neck for a moment. I feel like a bone fought over by two dogs. Dorit smiles at the sergeant. It's similar to the flirty smile she gave my brother, but this one doesn't reach her eyes.

"I was going to bring the colonel some coffee," she says. "If they have any of those chocolate wafers left, I'll bring you some."

The sergeant hesitates. He outranks her and could order her to leave. But the bribe works. He lets me go.

Dorit grabs each of us by the upper arm. Her long nails dig into my flesh. Beni yelps. She doesn't ease up. She marches us down the hallway and all but pushes us out the door.

"Can we have some chocolate wafers too?" I ask, just to tease her.

Dorit's face is pink, her mouth turned down in fury.

Not far from us, the door of a nondescript hut flies open and dozens of soldiers come pouring out, ripping gas masks off their faces. Some of them are retching, vomiting in the dirt. All of them have tear-streaked faces, snot pouring down.

"One of those guys is your brother," Dorit says coldly. "They're finishing up their chem drill."

"Why?" Beni asks, shocked. He swivels his head to get a better view, but Dorit keeps towing us toward the front gate.

"The Egyptians used poison gas in their last war in Yemen," she says as she herds us to the front gate. "We have to be prepared for them to use it on us too. For the drills, we put masks on as a tear-gas grenade is pulled. To practice remaining calm in the face of terror."

She lets those cold facts sink in. We're at the front gate.

"We're busy here," she says. "Don't ever try that stunt again." Then she hurries away.

As we walk back to the bus stop, I realize I still have Gideon's book in my pocket. Oh, well—he's probably too busy to read it anyway.

I try to remember every detail of our time on the base: the tough-looking soldiers, the cool radios and jeeps. Even Gideon's unit, racing out of the tear gas chamber, was everything I pictured military training would be like. I can't stop smiling. But when I look over at Beni, he doesn't share my excitement.

"That was a stupid idea," he says angrily. "My heart's still beating too fast. We could have gotten in big trouble!"

"It's no big deal," I tell him. "The worst part is that we're not getting any chocolate wafers. That fat sergeant is going to eat all of them." I figured that would make him smile, but he glares at me, as disapproving as any adult.

"I'm not really hungry anyway," he says sullenly, looking at his feet and kicking at the dry dirt. A few scraggly wildflowers shiver under a cloud of dust.

I feel a stab of guilt. I hadn't realized just how frightened Beni must've been. I forget sometimes that being six can be harder than being twelve. I take his hand.

We sit on the bench at the bus stop for half an hour. The sun cooks the black tar on the road, and shimmering waves of heat in the distance look like water. A mirage. I learned about mirage in school: a false vision, an illusion without substance.

"Don't worry, Beni," I tell him. "We're okay."

Our hands grow sweatier and sweatier, but neither one of us lets go.

Chapter Seven

More Bad News

It's just my luck that when we return home, Mrs. Friedburg is sitting on a chair in a patch of sun next to the building's front door.

"Motti! What are you doing? Why haven't you been home, helping your mother?"

"She's fine, Mrs. Friedburg," I say, hustling my brother through the front door. "She doesn't need me."

"Listen to you, Mr. Know-It-All. Your father is gone, Gideon is gone. The world's gone crazy. Yes, my boy, she needs you."

I feel hot color wash up my face.

"Go," she urges. "Help her, and don't cause trouble."

When Beni and I enter our apartment, I call out to my mom.

She's sitting in front of the radio, nervously smoking. She straightens with a guilty jolt when she hears us, stamping out the cigarette in the same saucer my father used as an ashtray.

"How was Gideon?" she asks. "Were you able to see him? Was he happy to get his book?"

Beni and I exchange looks.

"It was nice to see him," I say, evading the book question. "But he was very busy."

"We got to go on the base," Beni pipes up, too excited to hold back.

"What?" my mom exclaims.

"I had to poop, Ima, really badly!"

My mom bursts out laughing. "They let you in to use the facilities! Oh! Those sweet guys!"

It's been a while since I heard her laughing. Not since my dad was called up.

"All right, you silly boys. Motti"—she shoots me a look—"I hope you didn't make too much trouble. You know how busy they are on the base now."

I shake my head with sweet, innocent eyes.

"We just went in and Beni used the bathroom."

Her eyes narrow in sudden suspicion, so I change the subject fast. "We're so hungry. Can we eat early? I'll set the table."

She rises from her perch near the radio, turning the volume down, but not turning the radio off.

"That's a good idea. The prime minister is going to speak tonight about our next move," she says. "Maybe there will be some good news. Or at least some sort of decision. All this waiting is the worst part. Gives your imagination time to really go wild."

For the first time since my dad was mobilized, I'm glad he's not here. He would not have let me off so easily. My dad doesn't trust me as much as my mom does.

After a quiet meal with just the three of us, we take seats in front of the radio. By unspoken agreement, we leave my dad's orange chair empty. I finish up some schoolwork while Beni and my mom read a book together. The radio plays classical music softly. At the top of the hour, the radio beeps to signal a news update.

The Egyptian president Nasser announces that if Israel tries to send a ship to Eilat through the Straits of Tiran, he will consider it an act of war.

He has declared: "Under no circumstances will we allow the Israeli flag to pass through the Gulf of Aqaba. The Jews threaten war. We tell them: 'Ahlan Wa-sahlan *(You are welcome). This water is ours.'"*

When we listen to this latest broadcast, Beni turns to my mom. She's gripped the armrest of her chair so hard her knuckles have turned white.

"But we don't *want* war," he says in a small voice. "Doesn't he know that?"

"I know, sweet boy," my mom says, gathering him to her. He sits in her lap, his legs nearly reaching the floor. He's really too big to sit like that, but neither of them seems to care.

We stay tuned for Eshkol's speech.

"Finally," my mom murmurs, reaching for a fresh cigarette. I've never seen her smoke this much. "We need to know what comes next."

But her hopes do not last long. Eshkol's voice on the radio sounds worried. "The military continues to be alert," he says hesitantly.

Talk about stating the obvious.

"The government is reviewing reports from the foreign minister regarding his meetings with many states." He begins to list the various countries that have had meetings with our representatives. Even my mom, who was at the edge of her seat when the broadcast began, starts looking glazed with boredom.

Then he stops in the middle of a sentence, stutters, and mutters something under his breath in Yiddish. I picture him squinting and fiddling with his glasses. If the soldiers on the base were everything I pictured the military to be, our prime minister is everything he shouldn't be. We need a heroic leader, brave and bold. Instead, we have a shopkeeper with bad eyesight.

With the sea path to Eilat closed, with the UN peacekeepers dismissed, with our Western allies refusing to help us as Egypt and Syria gather massive forces at our borders and other Arab nations pledge support in the united cause of our obliteration, our prime minster explains that more meetings and discussions are on tomorrow's agenda. Instead of describing our nation's plans, he basically admits that our government can't decide what to do.

"*Oy vey,*" my mother says softly. A thin wisp of smoke from her cigarette slowly spirals upward. Our apartment falls silent. There's no sound coming from outside. It feels as if all of Jerusalem, the entire state of Israel, is stunned. What are we going to do?

"Ima," Beni says, resting his head on her plump shoulder, "do we have any gas masks at home?"

"What?" she asks in bewilderment. "Of course not! Why would you think that?"

"If Egypt attacks us with poison gas, what are we supposed to do?"

"No, sweetheart, no, they won't do that."

"They might," he says stubbornly. "They did it in Yemen. We saw Gideon practicing with his gas mask. But if we don't have one, what are we supposed to do—hold our breath?"

My mom shoots me a questioning look.

"On our way off the base we saw Gideon's unit coming out from a chem drill," I explain.

I'm pleased with the way that came out. I didn't lie, and I sounded kind of cool saying "chem drill."

"Oh," she says softly.

I suddenly realize that I've frightened her.

"Gideon was fine," I hurry to explain. "They only used tear gas, you know. It doesn't actually harm you."

"I know," she says softly. That's when I understand she isn't worried about Gideon in the drill. She's worried about what will happen to Gideon when it isn't a drill.

"All right, boys," she says, rising to her feet. "Fretting won't do a bit of good. There's school tomorrow and life goes on. Get ready for bed."

* * *

The next morning there's an article in the newspaper that rabbis in Tel Aviv have marked sections of the city parks as overflow cemeteries. The war that is surely coming will have such a high death toll that the city's cemeteries will not have enough room for all the bodies.

As I walk to school, there's a heavy tension in the air, like a rubber band that's being pulled tighter and tighter. It feels like something is going to snap.

* * *

Later in the day, large demonstrations erupt in Jerusalem. On the Jordanian side, Palestinians chant, "We want war!" The armies of Lebanon, Kuwait, and Saudi Arabia have activated and pledged to the fight. Iraqi troops and tanks are on the move toward Syria and Jordan to join the "battle of honor." Even some distant African nations that seem to have nothing to do with our fight in the Middle East—Sudan, Algeria, Morocco, and Tunisia—pledge troops and weapons to the Arab cause. Muslims all over the world seem to be united against us.

That afternoon's broadcast announces: *England has declined to support a preemptive attack by Israel. In the US, the president urges Israel to have "steady nerves" and not fire a shot.*

In related news, the Palestinian Liberation

Organization leader Shuqayri has declared: "We shall destroy Israel and its inhabitants, and as for the survivors—if there are any—the boats are ready to deport them."

It feels like the whole world is against us.

* * *

After the morning in school, crammed in Morah Pnina's class, I'm in a bad mood, itching to do something. I'm not the only one. Morah Pnina is starting to lose her voice from shouting at us so much. At lunch, my mom is distracted and short-tempered. We get a letter from my dad on army-issued green paper, but it doesn't say much. Only how nice it is to see all the guys from his old unit and that he misses us.

My mom pushes away her plate. She's hardly touched her rice and peas.

"I have a terrible headache," she says. "I'm going to lie down." Her skin is sallow and pinched. She's lost weight in the past two weeks, and it shows in her face.

"Okay, Ima, we'll be quiet," Beni says.

She smiles tiredly and pats his head. As she heads to the bedroom, I notice she grabs a pack of cigarettes and the nearly overflowing ash-tray/saucer. Somehow, I don't think she'll rest much. Beni clears the table while I get busy cleaning the kitchen. As soon as he's finished, he goes outside to play marbles with his friends in the shade of the massive eucalyptus tree in the courtyard.

As soon as I'm done washing and drying the dishes, I head out.

Yossi meets me at the field. His mom still doesn't want him playing with me. She thinks Yossi went to the library to study. We play soccer with the neighborhood kids, but no one plays with any heart. None of us are in the mood. There's a sour feeling in the air. Two boys end up in a fistfight over whether the ball was out or not. Yossi is unusually quiet.

I hear the chants long before I can make out any of the words.

"Come on," I say, eager to get away from the simmering tension on our field. "Let's check it out."

The rest of the boys follow me as we race through the streets. The voices get louder, angrier. In the square, hundreds of people, mostly women, are shouting. They're demanding the resignation of Prime Minster Eshkol. I don't know why they think it's better to have a brand new prime minister right before a war starts. But maybe they're just trying to say that they're scared and wish the situation were different.

"My mom's packing our suitcases, otherwise she would probably be here," Yossi says, looking straight ahead at the dark mass of women crowding the square.

"Huh?"

"We're leaving." His hands are shoved in his pockets, his skinny elbows tucked against his sides.

"You're going on a trip? Now?" His news is enough to completely take my mind off the demonstration. As long as I've known Yossi, he's never taken a trip. Neither one of us has ever left the country.

"I have an uncle who lives in Morocco," he says. "My dad's brother. He invited us to come stay with him. Because, you know." Yossi shrugs and gestures at the protest in front of us.

"You're going to Morocco?" I say stupidly. "That's crazy."

"It's not crazy," Yossi says tightly. "It's safer."

"Morocco?" I say again. "Safer for a Jew than Israel?"

Yossi shifts his eyes away, unable to meet my incredulous stare.

"Morocco is sending troops to fight us!" I remind him, feeling a hot wave of anger wash over me. "You think that's a safer place for you?"

"My mom says this is it." Yossi's shoulders hitch up higher as he pulls in his chin like a turtle. Like a stupid, frightened little turtle.

"She's totally wrong!"

Yossi doesn't answer, though he looks miserable.

"What if this is the end of Israel?" he asks in a low, choked voice. "Millions of Jews were murdered in the Holocaust, and no one saved them."

"We don't need anyone to save us," I say, full of bravado I don't really feel. "We'll save ourselves. My brother Gideon and the rest of the army will protect us."

"I hope so," Yossi says hollowly.

"When are you going?"

"Tomorrow," he says so quietly I can barely hear him. "There's a ship that leaves tomorrow."

I sway with shock. "When were you going to tell me?!"

"My mom only decided yesterday. Her cousin works next to the American Embassy in Tel Aviv. She told my mom the Americans all left. They know something," he says earnestly. As if we don't all know something. As if it isn't obvious.

"Who cares if the Americans are leaving?" I say, though I feel a heavy sinking in my stomach at the thought. "This isn't their country. But it is your country, and you're running away!"

"I'm not running away!" he yells back. "My mom's making me go!"

The protesters have marched on, their chants growing fainter. The rest of the neighborhood boys decide what to do now.

"Come on," says David, a tall sandy-haired

boy from my class. "Let's go back to the field. The score's tied."

"No, I want to see what they do next," says Moishe, short with a mop of dark, curly hair. "Maybe they'll storm the Knesset!" He's grinning like he hopes they will.

The boys split, some following the marchers, others heading back to the field. Yossi and I don't move. The air grows still and hot. The sun radiates off the white Jerusalem stone walls. Somewhere a bird trills the same three-note song over and over.

I don't know what to say. Yossi has been my best friend since we started school in first grade.

"I can't believe you're really leaving," I say.

"I can't believe it either," he says, his misery showing.

"Maybe you can stay with us," I offer. "You can have Gideon's bed, he's always at the base." For a moment I can picture it: Yossi moving in with us, Yossi at the table eating dinner with us.

But he shakes his head. "I have to stay with my mom," he says softly. "She's all alone, you know. I'm the only one she's got left."

Of course. I know that.

"So go," I say, half-shrugging. "I'll write you a letter and tell you what you missed."

"Motti," he says helplessly. "I'm sorry."

I can't stand this. I grab him in a rough hug. He wraps his arms around me in return. He smells like cumin and soap. I shut my eyes, breathing heavily through my nose. Then I push us apart and take off, running for home.

Chapter Eight
Drills

When I get home, my mom is in the living room holding a pair of sharp shears. There's a tangle of cloth at her feet. She looks up in surprise when I walk in.

"I didn't expect you back so soon."

"What are you doing?" I ask at the same time.

"Oh," she says. She looks at the pile at her feet as though surprised. "The radio said we should tape up the windows."

"Why?"

"If there's any bombing, the explosions will shatter the glass. If we tape them, then the glass will stick to the tape and just fall down. Otherwise, fragments could get blown in."

"Why the sheets?"

She smiles faintly. "An old trick I learned in '48. We don't have enough tape for the windows." I nod. I picture the small roll of clear tape we use for wrapping presents. Hard to imagine it doing much for us. "I'll cut the old sheets into strips. Then I'll dip them in flour and water and paste that to the windows." Her tone is reasonable and calm. Just a small lesson in physics and home economics.

Suddenly, a piercing siren screeches. I clap my hands over my ears, my heart racing.

"Has it started?" I shout. "Are we at war?"

My mom hurriedly sets down the sharp scissors. She glances at the clock on the wall.

"It's just a drill," she says quickly. "They announced it on the radio. Come on." She reaches for my hand. "Let's go to the shelter."

The younger boys playing outside rush back into the building, herded by Ofra Geffen. Some older buildings have to use a public shelter, but ours has a dedicated shelter in the basement. My mom yanks open the heavy metal doors, and we all tumble down a short flight of stairs and into the cement-walled shelter.

The shelter is dimly lit by a single naked bulb. It's cool and musty-smelling. In the corner, someone has piled boxes of supplies: bottled water, candy bars, dried fruit. There are candles and matches. A couple of covered buckets in case we're stuck long enough to need the bathroom.

Five minutes after we enter the shelter, the all-clear siren blares.

We walk out into the bright, warm sunshine. I look at my neighbors, blinking like owls in the sun. Only women, children, and old men. All the fathers and older brothers have gone to defend us. At moments like this, it all seems unreal. Is war really coming? Will bombs really fall on my street? I shiver, knowing that, ready or not, all that and more is coming our way.

* * *

Two nights later, Gideon surprises us, showing up in the middle of dinner.

"They let you come home?" my mom exclaims. She pushes back her chair from the table so hard that it topples over with a crash. She runs to him and pulls him down for a hard embrace.

"*Shalom*, Ima," Gideon says, half-laughing as he pats her back. "It's okay, don't worry."

"Come," she says. "Sit. Did you eat? Are you hungry?"

"Starving," he says. "They drill us so much, there's barely time to eat."

But he hasn't lost weight. He's tanned and looks fit. Having him at the table feels so wonderful, we're all chipper. Beni perks up and starts telling Gideon all about the crazy things the students and teachers found in his school's bomb shelter. Part of the school's shelter is the gymnasium, but for the last ten years, the back of it was used as a storage unit. Now that it needs to be a shelter again, they're clearing it out. Besides the usual old desks, water-stained textbooks, and broken musical instruments, a few teachers unearthed a food cache from before the 1948 War of Independence: crumbly old crackers, moldy dried beans, and bottled olive oil that went rancid long ago. Someone back then must have hidden the food before the war in case of shortages, like squirrels burying acorns, and then they forgot all about it.

It reminds me of how our little country has never been far from violence. These growing tensions are nothing new.

Gideon laughs. "And how's your tummy?" he asks Beni. "The guys keep teasing me about my brother with the runs."

Beni turns beet red.

"It wasn't like that—" he protests.

"Dorit has a crush on you," I say, to draw the attention off poor Beni. Plus, I really don't want my mom asking too many questions about what we did on base.

"Who's Dorit?" my mom asks, eyebrow raised.

Beni doesn't waste the opportunity. "Gideon has a giiiiirrrrrllllfriend," he sings.

Now Gideon's the one who's blushing. I sit back in satisfaction. I knew that would do the trick.

"Relax," Gideon says, more to my mom than to Beni. "Dorit's a sweetheart, but we're not dating."

My mom wiggles in her seat a bit. She loves to find out about Gideon's love life. Gideon's dated girls, but he hasn't had a serious girlfriend since he graduated high school.

"*Nu,* tell me a bit about her. Where is she from? Do I know her parents?"

Gideon rolls his eyes, and I laugh out loud. Gideon gives me a look, threatening retribution.

"Ima, I promise you," he says, "if I'm serious about someone, you'll be the first to know. But there's nothing there." He glares at me. I grin back. Everything about tonight feels so wonderful. Only my dad's empty chair at the table reminds me that it's not quite perfect.

Then, a miracle. Our apartment door opens again, and my dad walks in.

"Abba!" Beni screams and tears off toward him. My dad isn't even two steps into our home before Beni launches himself into his arms. My dad has fast reflexes, though. He grabs Beni and throws him in the air, as if Beni were three instead of six. Beni squeals with delight. Then my dad hugs him tightly and Beni buries his face in the crook of my dad's neck.

We all return to the table for a third time. There's still plenty of food, and we nibble second and third helpings as my dad fills his plate.

My dad's base is full of Jerusalem residents, and he knows half of them from his time in the military or from neighborhood interactions.

"Yakov Sitrin is in my platoon," he tells us around a mouthful of bread.

Yakov Sitrin is our mailman. A short, slim man, he always whistles as he pulls the handcart full of letters to deliver. I have a sudden, hilarious vision of him whistling and pulling a cannon behind him.

"Does he deliver everyone's mail on the base?" Beni asks.

With mailmen from all over the city serving in the military, high-school students have volunteered to deliver the mail. So many teens stepped forward that for the past week, we've received mail twice a day.

"No," my dad says. "He helps us hand out supplies and keep track of the inventory, like everyone else in the unit."

I can easily picture my dad repairing and

cleaning his weapon, helping out under the hood if a jeep breaks down. I have a harder time imagining him charging up a hill, firing his weapon, destroying instead of creating. Fortunately, his army job isn't a combat position.

"All this waiting is driving me crazy," Gideon says. "All we do is wait. The entire country is mobilized, and the politicians waste our one advantage."

"It's not that easy," my dad answers him carefully. "Young men rush into war, old men think about it a thousand times."

"We're going to war, Abba," Gideon says. "No one can doubt that. And if we don't strike first, we'll bleed a lot more."

After dinner, we all take an evening stroll. We cross King David Street and ride the elevator to the top of the YMCA Tower, the tallest structure in West Jerusalem. From the observatory deck we can see the golden half-egg top of the Dome of the Rock, the walls of the Old City, and the headlights of Jordanian cars driving on the streets just beyond the barbed wires of the border. Unlike Israeli West Jerusalem, they are not under a blackout. As twilight falls, our city doesn't light up like usual. Cars have painted their headlights dark blue, leaving only a thin strip clear for a bit of light. Windows are covered with thick shades, and the streetlights don't flicker on.

But though East Jerusalem is lit, the Western Wall remains unseen. Hidden behind the buildings of the Old City, we can only guess where it is from the few stones of the top rows. It is so close, yet impossibly far. Gideon grips the metal fence that runs along the observatory deck and stares at the Old City. A fierce look of longing crosses his face. A soft evening breeze tickles my hair. For some reason, I shiver, goose bumps rising on my arms.

After a few moments, Beni loses interest in the view. "Can we have ice cream?" he begs. It would be a real treat for my parents to buy us some.

"Yeah!" I second. "Please?"

My parents exchange amused glances. We all know this is a special night. "*Ooo-wah*," my dad says. "This is turning into a wild evening."

Beni and I grin, and even Gideon smiles.

The four of us stroll to the local ice-cream parlor, debating if our favorite flavors will be there. A few days ago my mom was assigned ration cards for staples like sugar and oil. It's so that people can't stock up on supplies and cause shortages for everyone else. We are the only customers at the ice-cream shop. They have all four flavors that they usually carry. We each order a different flavor, and everyone shares. Whether it's because of low demand or because the rationing works, I'm just glad that the shop has enough ingredients for its ice cream.

Once we get home, Beni falls asleep quickly. My parents hole up in the kitchen, feverishly talking in low voices.

Gideon and I sit on the couch by the radio.

The living room windows are open to catch the night breeze. The soft sounds of crickets and far-away cars drift in and keep us company. I feel very grown-up, staying up to chat with my brother—and at the same time, all the stress and fear of the past three weeks finally have some place to go.

"Yossi left," I tell him. "He and his mom are sailing to Morocco."

Gideon shakes his head. "I never did like that kid," he says.

"But what if his mom's right?" I say, hardly believing that I'm saying this out loud. "What if this is the next Holocaust? What if Arabs come and kill everyone? They keep saying that on the radio."

"Motti, we will win because we *must*," Gideon says fiercely. "The Egyptians fight for pride, for glory. The Syrians fight because they hate us. If they lose, so what? They can always try again. But us?" He taps his chest. "We fight for our families, our homes. We don't have another choice. Which is why we will win." He leans forward, putting an arm around my shoulders and pulling me toward him so we're nose to nose, eye to eye. "The soldiers fighting with me—you've never seen such patriots," he says. "Tough and smart. Real warriors."

The tight bands of panic around my chest slowly loosen. I understand what my brother is saying. He's saying they're like him. That we have brigades full of Gideons ready to do everything in their power to protect our homeland.

"No one wants war," he says. "But morale is so high on the base, Motti. Because if it comes to war, we *know* we will win."

I want to say, *Do you promise?* But I hold myself back. It isn't fair to ask him something like that. No one can promise me we'll win. Instead, I say, "Okay. How will we win?"

Gideon leans back, crossing an ankle over his knee.

"A long time ago, this army colonel, Chaim Laskou, figured out the five precepts—five laws, basically—of all Israeli wars. These things will always be true. One." He holds up a finger. "We will always be outnumbered. Two." Another finger. "We will never be able to keep a huge standing army, and we can never afford huge personnel losses. Three. We will always fight for our survival. If we lose, there won't be some treaty or cease-fire—there will just be no Israel. Four. We're a tiny country, 140 kilometers at our widest point, 15 kilometers at our narrowest. The Arab countries have the high ground.

We don't have any big rivers or mountains to slow their attacks."

I know all this, and I'm not sure how hearing it is supposed to make me feel better.

"Where's the part where you tell me how we're going to win?" I demand.

He holds up the last finger, showing me his whole wide palm before he bunches it into a massive fist. "Five. Because of these other factors, our wars must always be aggressive, fierce, and short." He smacks that fist into his open palm. I jump at the sound. "The problem so far has been that the world doesn't want to see us start the war. They don't want us firing the first shot. But a sudden, aggressive offense is our best defense. We've spent years getting ready for this, Motti. The Arabs are too busy practicing their victory parades to actually prepare for war."

My brother rises from the couch, and I follow.

"It's late," he says, stretching his arms over his head. I can hear his back popping as it aligns. "I have to be back at the base by seven tomorrow."

"I told Yossi he could come live with us," I tell him. "If he had accepted, he would have taken your bed."

Gideon snorts. "Thanks a lot, little brother. Already replacing me, eh?"

I shrug a shoulder. "It was worth a shot."

He shakes his head ruefully. I watch him head to the back bedroom.

"I'm kidding," I say, suddenly uneasy to joke about this. "You know that, right?"

Gideon turns, his brown eyes meeting mine.

"It'll be okay, Motti," he says kindly, answering my deepest, unvoiced fear. "We'll be fine."

Chapter Nine
The Queen of Sheba

In the morning Gideon and my dad return to their bases. My parents embrace in the hallway. My mom stands at our door, looking forlorn, as my dad and brother disappear down the cool, dark stairwell. Then she takes a deep breath and straightens her back, her chin tipping up. By the time she turns to come back into our apartment, she's composed.

"All right, boys," she says, clapping her hands at us like we're ducks dilly-dallying on the path. "Get your shoes on, brush your teeth, pack your books. School starts in twenty minutes."

My mom is a tough lady. She was twenty-three years old during the 1948 War of

Independence. Gideon had just been born. When he was three days old, the clinic where he was born was shelled. My mom had been there, recovering from the labor, but suddenly she had to move. She grabbed her new baby and fled into the streets, barefoot. My dad was fighting the Jordanians in Jerusalem. My grandparents' apartment was too far away for her to run there.

When my mom tells us the story, she makes it sound like a crazy adventure. Wearing only a nightgown, she ran into an abandoned warehouse and wedged herself in a corner. She sang lullabies to Gideon, rocking him and kissing his little face. He slept through the whole thing, utterly unperturbed by the explosions that shook the ground or the shots ringing out in the streets.

I used to find that so hilarious, that baby Gideon slept through a war.

On my way to school, I pass a large dump truck. I stop to watch as it opens its rear door and a mass of sand pours out. Two men hop out of the front cab and drop a pile of empty bags next to the sand. Then they hop back in the truck and roar away.

A milling group of men with shovels—men from the Civil Defense, men who are too old to be called up to active duty—start filling the empty sacks with sand.

One of them notices me watching.

"There's no points for spectators, boy," he says roughly. "Grab a scoop and start filling."

School starts in a few minutes, but I suddenly get the feeling that I won't be making it in today. Between Morah Pnina teaching eighty kids and Yossi heading to the port in Haifa to catch the ship to Morocco, no one will even notice I'm not there. So I grab an empty bag and start filling it. I tie it off and drop it on the growing pile.

Once we have a mound of sandbags, the men get organized in a line leading from the pile to the entryway of the nearest apartment building. I take my place in the line. We pass each bag from person to person, making a chain across the street. The sandbags are laid in rows along the windows and the entryway, making a small wall of blast protection.

When we've used all the sand the dump truck dropped off, some of the men stay to dig a trench. I follow the others as we walk toward the next sand drop site to fill more bags.

People come out of their apartments. Mothers and grandmothers, little children. Other kids skipping school like me. At the next dump site, a few of us climb to the top of the mound, a mini-mountain. I get a brilliant idea.

"Watch this!" I call. I take two running steps and launch myself off the edge of the hill. I land on my bottom and slide the rest of the way down, whooping the whole way.

"Me next!" calls another boy and does the same thing.

The adults stop to watch our antics.

"Enough!" calls an older lady. She's wearing a kerchief on her hair and a long skirt to her calves. Orthodox. "You're making a mess of the sand. Start helping out, not making more work."

The boys and I exchange sheepish looks. For a moment, I almost forgot why we were here. It feels nice to have everyone out, in each other's business, working together.

We fill the empty sacks. Once all the sand is used, we form a new line to hand the bags from the street to the building's entryway and windows. I take a bag, turn to hand it to the person next to me. I freeze.

The man waiting for the sandbag in my hands is a black man wearing loose white robes and a soft white hat. He must be one of the priests from the Ethiopian monastery near our neighborhood. Jerusalem is full of churches, convents, and monasteries, some nearly a thousand years old. There are many types of Christian sects here—each faction of priests, monks, and nuns wearing distinctive robes that distinguish them from the others.

There isn't usually much mingling between the priests and the locals. They keep to themselves, and we stay out of their way. The priest notices my hesitation. He smiles, bright white teeth flashing in his dark face.

"It's all right," he says in softly accented Hebrew. "All the neighbors are here to help."

My heart swells with sudden happiness. Maybe the whole world *isn't* against us.

My priest and I work hard. After we finish with this sand mound, we walk together to the next one. And the next.

By lunchtime we're both sweaty and exhausted.

"Come, friend," he says. He has a lilting accent that I find charming. It's nothing like the sharp sounds of Europeans or the slippery inflection of immigrants from the Middle East. "Let us eat."

"I can't," I say, wiping my hand across my face. Gritty dirt and sand itch on my sweaty skin. "My mom expects me home for lunch. She'll worry if I don't show up. She doesn't even know I'm not at school today."

"I see. Have you time for tea, then?" he asks, unperturbed. He's been like that all morning. Calm and unhurried, though he worked steadily and efficiently, never slowing down, never wasting motion.

I'm so parched my throat feels like sandpaper.

"That would be great," I say. "She won't mind if I'm a few minutes late."

I follow him to the monastery compound. The top of the gated entrance has a crest with a lion on it. We pass through the gate into an open courtyard. There are several priests there, sitting at tables under the shade of large palm trees. Several women, their hair covered with wispy white cotton scarves, serve the men with trays of tea and food.

One of the women approaches us with a tray. She looks about my mother's age, with high cheekbones and a round, friendly face. The white shawl covering her hair and shoulders flutters in the slight breeze. I take one of the small glasses of dark amber tea from the tray. It isn't kosher. My mom would say that I shouldn't drink it. But I smile as I inhale the scents of cinnamon and cloves mingling in the steam that softly curls up from my cup.

I take a small sip, too curious about this African tea to pass up the chance to taste it. Sweet and rich—delicious. Though it's hot, it glides down my throat and quenches my thirst.

"Thank you," I say. "It's very good."

"Yes," he nods. He sips from his own glass.

He sighs with pleasure. "On hot days, it's good to drink hot tea."

I give him a confused look. "That doesn't make sense," I say.

"But it is true," he says. "My people know about hot days. There are things in life that do not seem . . ." He hesitates, searching for a word. ". . . like they belong together, but they do. Like me and you. We are connected."

"Because we live in the same neighborhood?" I ask.

"Yes. But more so than that. Do you know the story of my people?"

I shake my head. I have no idea why there are African priests living in my neighborhood. I always accepted it because I was used to seeing them, but I suddenly wonder what drew them here.

"The *Kebra Nagast* is one of our holy books, nearly a thousand years old. It tells how the Queen of Sheba came to visit Jerusalem in the time of King Solomon. She was very clever, the queen. Very wealthy. Very beautiful."

The other priests have settled down for their

lunch. They tear pieces from a thin pancake and use it to scoop lentils and cooked vegetables. They're eating, but I can tell they are also listening to my priest's story.

"The queen had heard tales of King Solomon's great wisdom. She was curious to meet this special king. So she traveled all the way from Ethiopia to Jerusalem. Imagine, a journey of more than two thousand kilometers, through the burning desert of Arabia. She brought with her thousands of servants, and camels with heavy loads of rare spices, jewels, and gold." He gestures with his dark, strong hands, his fingers long and tapered, a magician conjuring the image of a long caravan and endless sand dunes. I can picture it: a tall regal queen, swaying under a jeweled canopy, shading her eyes against the glare.

"She traveled for six months to meet the king, and when she did, she had many riddles to test his wisdom. He answered them all."

I study the Bible at school—it's part of the standard curriculum. So I already know this story. I read the section in Kings where the

Queen of Sheba visits King Solomon. It's a boring little part that I could barely stay awake for. I am curious to hear how this relates to the Ethiopian priests.

"The queen noticed the fine clothes that King Solomon and his attendants wore. She saw how everyone listened to King Solomon and hurried to obey his wise commands. Miracles happened before her eyes. And she ate the food, which was spicier than anything she had ever tasted.

"King Solomon invited her to spend the night in his palace. She accepted. Then he asked her to marry him." My priest pauses. "But she said no. The king told her he would never force her. He vowed that it would only happen by her own choice. If she came to him at night when he was lying in his bed, that would mean she had decided to be his wife. The queen agreed to this, knowing she would never go into his bedchamber. But that night she woke up terribly thirsty. The spicy food, you see, made her desperate for water."

I stare into my teacup. My watery reflection

looks back at me. This isn't how the story about the Queen of Sheba goes in the section of Kings that I read. In Kings it only says that the Queen of Sheba came and that she was impressed by how smart and rich King Solomon was. There's nothing about tricks or getting married. But the priest's story doesn't sound wrong. I can picture the clever king doing anything it takes to get his way.

"There was no water anywhere," the priest says. He takes a sip of his tea, as if to highlight how thirsty the queen must have been. "She called to her servants, but they told her the only water to be found was beside the king's bed. She resisted as long as she could, but she was dying of thirst. Finally, she rushed to the king's chamber. She poured water from a pitcher by his bed and drank deeply. Suddenly, the king sat up!" My priest opens his eyes wide, acting the scene. He's a wonderful storyteller. "He had been awake the whole time. 'You came into my bedchamber,' he said. 'According to our bargain, we are now married.' Nine months later she had a son, Menelik the First. The son of his son of his son down the generations is the king of Ethiopia to this day. There are Ethiopian Jews who live in my country today, descendants of this alliance between the Queen of Sheba and the King of the Jews."

I'm pretty sure my eyes are as wide as plums. It would've been a lot easier to stay awake in Bible class if this were the story we learned.

"You see, my friend, we are all joined together. Our ancestors are your ancestors." He points to the lion motif above the gate. "This lion on our shield is from the banner that King Solomon gave to the Queen of Sheba. It is the Lion of Judah."

I pass this monastery often. I've seen that lion on the shield above the gate, and it never once occurred to me that it could be the Lion of Judah. I must look astonished.

The priest's brown eyes dance in mirth.

"We look so different, you and I," he says. "We sound and dress so differently, but we are connected through time."

The priest takes my empty teacup and smiles at me.

"Go home to your mother now," he says. "Do not cause her worry."

"Thank you," I say. "For the tea. And the story."

"It was my pleasure."

Then I turn and hurry home. I'm late for lunch.

Chapter Ten
Irony

I wake up in the middle of the night in a sudden rush, not sure what's wrong. The room is pitch black, our window covered in a thick blanket that doesn't let in even a bit of moonlight.

"Motti," my little brother moans. "Motti, I had an accident."

I fumble with my sheet and feel my way to the wall switch. I blink until my eyes adjust to the sudden light.

Beni sits in bed, sodden sheets twisted around his legs. The sharp smell of urine fills the room.

"Oh, Beni," I say in sleepy annoyance. "Come on, you're not a baby."

"I had a bad dream. Our house caught on fire and Ima burned up," he says and starts to cry. I shiver at the image.

"All right, all right," I say crossly. "There's no need to fall to pieces. Come on." I pull him out of bed. "Go to the bathroom and strip off the wet pajamas and wash your legs. I'll deal with the bed."

He waddles down to the bathroom, keeping his wet legs apart.

I stare at the mess on the bed. It's not just a little stain—he really wet it. I make a face as I grab a handful of wet sheet. When I pull it off the bed, I see that it's soaked through. There's a large wet circle on the mattress.

I go to the bathroom, wet a towel, and scrub out the stain. When Beni comes back to the room, he pulls on a fresh pair of pajamas and then hugs his middle as we both look at his wet bed.

"You can sleep in Gideon's room," I say.

"I don't want to sleep there," Beni says in a small voice. He's wearing my old pajamas with green trucks on them. His skinned knees and knobby feet remind me how young he is. I forget sometimes.

"Fine. Then I'll sleep there and you can have my bed."

Beni pokes out his lower lip and stares at the floor.

"What?" I sigh. "It's late. I want to go back to sleep."

"I don't want to sleep by myself," he finally says in a tiny voice.

I think about it. "You want to squeeze in with me?"

His face lights up.

"Okay," I say. I can't help smiling back. You'd think I'd offered him the moon. "But you have to promise not to kick!"

"Of course," he vows.

A thought occurs to me.

"And if you pee in my bed, Beni," I warn, "I get Gideon's bed and you're sleeping on the floor!"

Beni draws himself up.

"I never wet the bed twice in one night," he says with dignity.

"Good. So come on, I'm tired."

It takes us a little while to settle in comfortably, two boys in one narrow bed. But finally we find our comfy spots. I fall asleep with the warmth of my little brother tucked inside the curve of my chest and knees. His soft breaths keep me company, even in my dreams. Neither one of us has nightmares.

* * *

The next morning I skip school again. Our neighborhood is already fully equipped with sandbags, so I drift into the next section of town and help out.

Today, in addition to the Civil Defense men and boys like me, we have three tall, blond Germans. We keep sneaking glances at them. They were dropped off in a small van that didn't stay around. A lady just stuck her head out of the rolled-down window and shouted that they were volunteers and that she would be back to pick them up in the afternoon. They clearly want to help, but they don't speak Hebrew and no one in our group knows any German. The older men especially have their shoulders tight and faces grim, unwilling to even try to communicate with the foreigners.

"I'll be right back," I say and scamper back to my building.

"Mrs. Friedburg," I say when she opens the door, "we need a translator."

* * *

"They're volunteers," Mrs. Friedburg explains to us after chatting with them.

"So they say," says one of the Civil Defense men, sliding a suspicious sideways look at the tall, strapping Germans. "Boys like that ran my mother out of her house in Krakow, forced her on a cattle train to Auschwitz, and then killed her and my baby sister. If you think I'm turning my back on them, you have another thought coming."

"*Ach*," Mrs. Friedburg snorts. "These boys are here to help, and you're a fool if you don't take them up on their offer."

She sets them up with shovels and instructions. The three muscular young men happily get to work, laughing and joking in their deep voices. Apparently, while foreign governments are distancing themselves from our situation, young people from all over the world are coming in droves to personally help. The Germans tell Mrs. Friedburg that they are staying at a hostel with hundreds of Swedish, Canadian, and American volunteers.

Mrs. Friedburg beams at the Germans. They have icy blue eyes and fair skin that has reddened in the sun. Their rapid German banter makes the others uncomfortable. But I have to give them this, they work hard. Compared to the old men of the Civil Defense and the school boys like me, they fly through the sand mound, filling the bags faster than people can carry them to the windows and doors.

"So an American, a Brit, and an Israeli are hiking in the wild when they're caught by cannibals," says one of the Civil Defense men, taking a break as he leans against the handle of his shovel. The German volunteers eye him, but they continue with their work. "The cannibals throw them all in a giant pot. They're going to eat them. Their chief says, 'You can each have one last request.' The American asks for a glass of whiskey. The Brit says, 'I want a cigar.' The Israeli says, 'I want you to punch me in the face.' The chief says, 'What kind of request is that?'"

I know this joke. A different Civil Defense man told it to me yesterday.

"The Israeli says, 'That's the only thing I want.' Finally, the chief agrees, and he punches him in the face. The Israeli pulls out a gun and shoots the chief. The American and the Brit turn to him and say, 'You had a gun all along? Why didn't you just use it?' And the Israeli says, 'What? And have the UN accuse me of being the aggressor?'"

The Israelis all laugh. The Germans exchange looks. Mrs. Friedburg rushes to translate. A look of dawning comprehension crosses their faces. They snort in amusement. The man who told the joke beams at them, and they smile back.

Then one of them says something in German, looking earnestly at all of us. We all turn to look at Mrs. Friedburg.

"He says yes, that's why they're here."

After that, everyone is much easier around each other.

When we finish all the sand piles, Mrs. Friedburg invites the Germans to her apartment for lunch. I walk with them through the quiet streets. There are hardly any cars, and many stores are closed now that the people needed to work them are stationed along our borders. All the windows are covered with tape and blackout covers. Sandbag walls are everywhere.

The newspaper wrote that it costs Israel $20 million a day in lost economic revenue to keep so many people active in the reserves. For a little country like ours that was already struggling with a weak economy and a lot of unemployment, that's money we can't afford. It's one of the five precepts that Gideon explained to me. We can't afford to keep a large standing army. If Egypt and Syria just kept us mobilized long enough, the country would collapse without a single shot fired. Which means that the war that's coming our way will be here sooner rather than later.

The Germans chat and laugh, clearly happy

to be here. It seems strange to me that twenty-five years ago, young Germans like them killed millions of Jews and now, young Germans are here to help us.

"The German government has just donated twenty thousand gas masks," Mrs. Friedburg tells me as we walk, as if reading my mind.

"That's just ironic," I say. I expect her to jump down my throat. She doesn't like it when people insult Germany, the center of culture and learning.

But instead she just pats my back. "Motti," she says, "it's a gift for me to live to see this day."

She has a contented, peaceful look that I've never seen on her before. All these years she's held onto her pride and affection for Germany despite the terrible things that happened there. It couldn't have been easy. These three young Germans had just given her back something that an army of three million took away from her: true pride in her native country.

"But what about the situation?" I ask. Threats keep flying our way over the radio airwaves, and foreign troops have continued to pour into the

Sinai and Jordan, swelling their armed forces, which already outnumbered us ten to one. "Everyone knows that war is coming."

People are calling it *ha-mamtanah*, the wait. The entire country on edge, knowing that war's coming. Every day the pressure building, like a balloon that grows bigger and a little bigger, the thin skin stretched so tightly, and you know that soon, it's going to blow.

"Mark my words," she assures me. "Jordan won't enter the war. King Hussein is a reasonable, educated man. He knows there's no future in war with Israel. It's only the Syrians and the Egyptians we have to worry about." She pauses, considering. "And the Iraqi brigades. But not Jordan."

I think of my Jordanian soldier, the one who gave me candy and always winks at me. I think about my dad's childhood friend, Daoud. And then I remember the skinny Jordanian soldier with the dark glint in his eyes who aimed his rifle at me. I wonder which one is more like King Hussein.

Part II
The War

Chapter Eleven
June 5, 1967

As we eat breakfast that morning, the air is suddenly split by the screaming jets of fighter planes roaring low overhead. I drop my fork and race to the window, pushing aside the heavy blanket that blocks my view. I search the sky. But the planes are long gone.

My mom and I exchange looks.

"Do you think this is war?" I ask. I glance over at Beni. He's gone pale. He puts down his bread and puts an uneasy hand over his stomach.

"Could be training runs," my mom says. She speaks calmly, but I hear the tension in her voice. "There aren't any air raid sirens. Turn on the radio."

I do. But there's no news.

"You're going to school," my mom tells us. She levels me a look. "I mean it, Motti. No skipping."

A few days ago, dear Mrs. Friedburg just had to mention to my mom that I've been filling sandbags during school hours. My national defense days were abruptly cut short. My mom said I could help out after school, but not during school. This is the problem with Mrs. Friedburg. She is completely untrustworthy.

A few minutes later Beni and I are on our way to school. As we cross a narrow alley, a white flash passes in front of us. It's that green-eyed cat. It easily leaps on top of a metal trash can, and from there it bounds to a balcony crowded with potted plants. It balances gracefully along the balcony's wrought iron railing, and then pauses to look at me over its shoulder.

"Did you see that?" I exclaim.

Beni looks up from his feet, looking at me and then all around.

"What? What are you talking about?" he asks.

I point toward the balcony and the acrobatic cat. But it's gone. The balcony's empty.

Beni meets up with several boys from our street, and they walk the next eight blocks to his grammar school together. I turn at the corner and head to my school.

I'm sitting on the floor of Morah Pnina's classroom, my back resting against the door, when the air raid siren suddenly wails. Everyone freezes. A few students start to gather their things.

"Leave your things," Morah Pnina roars over the noise. "This isn't a drill."

Everyone rushes to their feet. Several chairs tip over and fall with a clatter.

"To the shelter!" she yells. "Now!"

I scramble to my feet as eighty kids come surging toward me. I fumble with the doorknob. Finally, it gives, and the door flies open. I stumble out of the classroom, my books and papers on the floor instantly trampled under dozens of feet. As soon as I step into the corridor, I'm carried along by the press of people. I couldn't turn around and go back to the classroom even if I wanted to. There's organized chaos as everyone races toward the shelter near the school yard.

Two teachers stand by the heavy metal door and urge students in. The siren wails and wails. Kids fly inside, stumbling over each other, plunging down the stairs into the dimly lit space. I focus on the open doorway of the shelter. My vision narrows until all I see is the dark rectangle of safety that beckons me. The siren screams, drowning out the shouts of the teachers, the cries of the students. My heart knocks painfully against my chest.

This is it. That thought plays over and over in my mind. *This is it. This is it.*

I make it into the shelter and find a place to sit on the damp, musty floor. The last student rushes in, the teachers duck inside and pull the blast-proof metal door closed. It shuts with a clang.

They are barely down the stairs when the first explosion hits. The ground shudders.

A few people scream.

It's followed by more explosions, some loud and nearby, others fainter and farther away. I try to keep track how many, but I lose count. The teachers huddle in a corner, fiddling with a transistor radio someone thought to bring along.

The radio crackles to life, but I can't hear it over the cries of the scared students.

"Children," Morah Pnina cries, trying to get control of the room. "Children, stay calm. Be quiet!"

But not even our strong-willed teacher can calm the crowd. I make my way over to the transistor, stepping over huddled students. I need to hear what's going on.

The teachers have turned the dial to Kol Israel, the official Israeli radio station. But it only plays music.

Morah Pnina turns the dial. Radio Cairo blasts in Hebrew: *Arise! Go forth to battle! The hour of glory is here! Our airplanes and our missiles at this moment are shelling all Israel's towns and villages.*

She turns the dial again. Radio Damascus reports: *Silence the enemy! Destroy him! Liberate Palestine! The Syrian air force has begun to bomb Israeli cities and to destroy its positions.*

Changing stations again, I hear King Hussein, speaking on Radio Amman, say: *The hour of revenge has come.*

"It's Jordan," Morah Pnina says in a flat voice. "King Hussein has thrown his lot in with Nasser."

It's the worst possible news. Little Israel, only nineteen years old, is now fighting a war on three fronts against three different armies, at the same time.

I think bitterly of Mrs. Friedburg's assurances. I should have known better than to believe her.

I suddenly picture Yossi, far away in Morocco. All the people who forecasted doom and death. With a horrible sense of realization, I see that they were right. A rising wave of terror like nothing I've ever felt before washes over me. War has come to Jerusalem. And with it, perhaps, the end of our Jewish country. And our lives.

Another explosion rattles the ground.

The teachers have all served in the military. They discuss the possibility of invasion by Jordanian ground troops. Shelling West Jerusalem is one thing. Bad, of course, but nothing compared to the utter slaughter of ground troops going house to house. There are also Egyptian and Iraqi troops currently in Jordan as part of a joint-forces agreement. Both the Jordanians and the Iraqis have particularly fearsome reputations, well-trained and lethal. And the border is not even a ten-minute walk from our school.

As if in agreement with the teachers' grim predictions, another explosion goes off. We all instinctively duck and cover our heads as the ground trembles around us.

I can't stand the thought of being stuck in my school's bunker when my mom is at home by herself. I have to get to her.

"Morah Pnina," I say, "I need to go home."

"No," she says. "Absolutely not." She turns to one of the pale, bug-eyed teachers next to her. "Open the boxes with the chocolate bars. Pass them out. It'll give the students something to distract them. Right now, we can all use the sugar."

"Morah Pnina," I try again.

"Here," she says and shoves a box of candy bars at me. "Take one."

"But," I say, holding the box, "I don't—"

"Motti, it would be suicide to leave the bunker right now." Morah Pnina is quite tall for a woman and the top of her head nearly brushes the ceiling. She hunches down, looming over me. The dim light casts long shadows on her face. "I know you want to go home. But your mom will kill me if I let you go now. As soon as there's a lull in the shelling, you can leave. Okay? But right now, help me get these students calm. Some of them are hyperventilating. Give them a candy bar."

I slip one of the bars in my pocket and make my way to my friends. I plop down and hand the box over to David. He reaches in, grabs a bar, and passes the box down. I much prefer to worry about my mom than to think about Gideon and my dad. I hope Beni is doing okay. It tears me up a little to think of him so scared in his school's bunker as the shells explode. Beni has my old teacher Morah Rivkah. I always liked her. She'll keep a cool head under pressure. I hope she keeps an eye on Beni.

I don't have a watch, but Moishe does. An

hour passes. Then another. I can't keep still. We finish the chocolate bars. Some kids eye the boxes of sweet crackers, but Morah Pnina holds them off.

"We need to pace ourselves," she says. What she means is, *We don't know how long we'll be stuck here, so let's not eat all the food in a couple of hours.*

Time moves achingly slowly. Again and again, there are rumbles of explosions. More jets fly overhead. Morah Pnina catches my eye and shakes her head no. I can't leave. Not yet.

We sit. We wait. We listen to the radio for news.

After six hours, I've had it. I feel ill from too much chocolate and sitting still for so long. My mind races with worries for my mom. She's probably beside herself with worry. None of her boys is with her. Not one.

I weave between the tight groups of kids to get over to the teachers. They sit leaning against the rough cement-brick wall, lost in their own world of worry.

"There hasn't been any shelling for half an hour," I tell her.

She shakes her head no. "The all-clear hasn't sounded," she says.

"Let me run home," I say. "I can be there in three minutes flat. Less if I really sprint."

Morah Pnina hesitates, thinking.

"I have to go," I tell her. "I'm going crazy."

She rubs a hand across her face. She lowers it and searches my face.

"Okay," she nods, looking pale. "You can go. Listen up," she says, raising her voice. "Anyone who lives in the immediate neighborhood, two or three minutes away at the most: If you want to run home, you can right now. You do not *have* to go. But if you want, you can."

A frightened hush falls over the crowd. I can see the kids who live nearby frantically thinking whether they want to risk it or not.

"Make a decision now," Morah Pnina says, anxiety sharpening her voice. "I'm opening the door for exactly thirty seconds."

I walk to the door, my heart thumping hard and fast. I bounce on my toes, ready to sprint for my life. I look over my shoulder. Most of the kids have stayed put, but David and Moishe, along with a couple of kids from the other grades, have come forward.

Morah Pnina nods. "Good luck," she says. "*Chazak v'amatz.*" Be strong and brave. It's an ancient blessing given by Moses to the Israelites before they crossed the Jordan River. We've studied it in her class. She unlatches the door and pushes it open. Sun streams in—just another sunny day in June.

"Go!" she says. "Run!"

We do.

At first we're all packed in, jostling through the door and out into the school yard. Then we scatter, five kids running in all directions, sprinting for home.

I race through the narrow streets that I strolled down just this morning. There's not a soul out. The sounds of my pounding feet and whistling breath are the only signs of human life. They echo off the buildings. The blue skies seem to mock me. The silence feels ominous.

Every second I'm out in the open is reckless. I run like I've never run before. The street seems to stretch out, like in a nightmare, getting longer and longer. I pump my arms, leaning forward. A building has been hit and rubble is strewn in the street. I clamber over it, quick and light on my feet. The laundry lines have snapped. Shirts and underwear hang down the side of the building like wilted leaves on a vine. Glass shards glitter and flash on the ground like a field full of diamonds. Suddenly, there's a scream of jet engines. It's so loud I feel it vibrating in the soles of my feet and up my legs.

Four Mirage jets shoot overhead, flying in a tight diamond formation. Without meaning to, I come to a stop, amazed to see them. The Israeli Air Force emblem, a blue star in a white circle, winks for a second on their wings before they're gone.

I blink, standing in the empty street.

Then I take off again, running as fast as I can.

Chapter Twelve
Fog of War

All the west-facing windows in my apartment building are shattered, though the building itself seems fine. I run under the shadow of the eucalyptus tree in our courtyard. I grew up playing in the shade of that tree while my mother sat nearby with the other moms, peeling potatoes or doing laundry in large vats of soapy water, gossiping, and laughing. My earliest memory is of spitting out a dried eucalyptus leaf because I'd thought it was a cracker.

As I tear up the walkway, glass crunches and grinds under my feet. I push through the front door and race to the basement stairs that lead to our bomb shelter. There are smears of red paint on the floor. My heart clenches at the sight. It's not red paint. It's blood.

I pound on the heavy metal door.

"It's Motti," I shout. "Let me in!"

For a few seconds nothing happens. Then I hear the clangs of the thick metal bolt sliding open. The door opens up. Mrs. Friedburg blinks at me in surprise.

"Ima!" I shout around her. "Ima, are you okay?"

Mrs. Friedburg steps aside. My mom scrambles to her feet. She's holding Yoram, Ofra Geffen's baby.

"Motti," she screams and runs toward me, still holding the baby. "Oh, my God! How did you get here?" She grabs me with one hand and pulls me into the shelter just as a rumbling explosion thunders again.

Mrs. Friedburg shuts the door behind me and I'm home.

My apartment building's shelter is smaller than my school shelter. Even though there are fewer people, we're all packed in. Efraim and Miriam Pinsky, the elderly couple from upstairs.

Shlomo, another older man who lives above us, and Mrs. Friedburg. Ofra Geffen and her two younger children. Shira is stuck at her all-girls school, which isn't far from Beni's school.

Esther Geffen, Shira's little sister, can't stop crying. She's sprawled on her mom's lap, wailing hysterically. Her mom is injured.

"Ofra's leg was badly gashed by flying glass," my mom tells me in a low voice. "The first siren caught them by surprise. They didn't make it down the stairs before a shell hit. The windows shattered." She makes a helpless gesture. "At least the baby's okay."

Ofra had tucked baby Yoram inside her shirt and curled around him as the windows exploded.

They've wrapped her leg in white gauze, but the blood seeps through. The sight of it has unhinged four-year-old Esther. It gives me the willies too. Esther raises a tear-streaked face, which is dotted with cuts. Her bare arms and legs have cuts too. She didn't escape unscathed.

The baby fusses and my mom coos over him. He whimpers. She jiggles him on her knees, but that upsets him. He lets out a wailing scream that has everyone in the room wincing.

"Who's a beautiful boy?" my mom croons in a calm singsong. "Who's so big and strong?" He smacks his little lips and she gives him her knuckle to suck on. Baby Yoram goes to town, sucking with all his might. No one brought a bottle for him.

I realize what a blessing it was when three-day-old Gideon slept through the shelling from the War of Independence. There's something terribly infuriating about a crying baby when everyone is stressed and scared. I want to scream, *Shut up!* Except that it won't do any good. I'm impressed by how calm my mom is. It must be so strange for her, like time folding back on itself. Another war, another bomb shelter, another baby in her lap.

Someone used the covered bucket before I got here. The whole room smells like raw sewage.

There's a small transistor radio crackling with news. None of it is good. Kol Israel remains mum about the situation. But Syria's President

Atassi announces, This battle will be one of the final liberation from imperialism and Zionism . . . We shall meet in Tel Aviv." On Radio Cairo, broadcasting in Arabic and Hebrew, we hear that the Israeli Air Force has been destroyed and that tanks are rolling into Tel Aviv.

This sets Esther wailing again. Her mom is pale and sweating with pain. My mom and I exchange looks. The baby sucks desperately on her knuckle. The mood in our dank, stinking shelter is bleak and hopeless.

"Nonsense," Mrs. Friedburg suddenly declares. Everyone looks at her as if she's lost her mind. "*Ach*," she says, waving her hand as if to banish this dark talk. "When the Voice of Berlin tells me something, I believe it. Turn off that terrible racket," she commands Shlomo, who sits by the transistor. He looks at her, slack-mouthed. "Immediately! We need happy voices now. When I was hidden for two years in a closet in godforsaken Augsburg, I sang to myself. Silently. Now, we will sing with all our strength!"

This is a new side to Mrs. Friedburg. Not daring to disobey, Shlomo clicks off the transistor.

Mrs. Friedburg starts us off with "*Hine Ma Tov*," a traditional hymn with an upbeat tune: *Behold, how good it is for brethren to dwell together in unity.*

At first it's only her voice that rings out. She has a clear, strong voice. My mom joins in, swaying with the baby. Then Shlomo with a passable baritone. Then me, then Esther and her mom. The Pinskys. We all sing it. The baby falls silent, staring at us with wide eyes. He looks so astonished that I fizzle with laughter. My mom looks at me with a warm, fond look. Baby Yoram rests his head on her comfortable bosom, snuggling in.

As soon as we finish, Mrs. Friedburg launches into "*Modeh Ani*." After that, everyone has ideas. I teach them Scout campfire songs. Shlomo teaches us an old Romanian lullaby. Ofra sings a breathy Persian love song.

I look at Mrs. Friedburg with new respect. She singlehandedly changed the mood for everyone in our shelter. She made us hopeful and less afraid. Maybe my dad was right. She really is some kind of hero.

During a lull in the shelling, I offer to race upstairs and bring back a milk bottle and extra nappies for the baby. The music no longer amuses Yoram, and he has started crying again. I can't really blame him this time. The unpleasant smell coming from his bottom would make anyone cry.

Ofra looks at my mom with questioning eyes, silently asking her if that's okay.

"Quick, quick, quick!" my mom urges me. Mrs. Friedburg holds open the thick shelter door, and I fly out. When I'm back less than three minutes later, the whole room erupts in applause and cheers. As my mom plugs the baby's mouth with the full bottle, everyone sighs with relief.

We pass around the bottled water and candy bars that we put in the shelter weeks ago. Shlomo trots upstairs and returns with a plastic bag full of plums that he hands out. By mutual silent agreement, my mom and I don't talk about Gideon or my dad. It's easier to worry about Beni. But I remind my mom about Morah Rivkah. We agree he's in good hands.

We sing more songs. Mrs. Friedburg lets Shlomo turn on the radio, but only if he keeps it tuned to Kol Israel. It plays music. There are no news updates.

At one point I hear Esther say to her mom, "I know why there's only music."

"Why, *motek*?" Ofra asks absently.

"So we won't be scared."

Ofra kisses the top of her little girl's head. We all know she's right.

It isn't until that evening that Kol Israel stops playing music. General Herzog begins to speak.

The fog of war is covering the battlefield, and it is more of an obstacle to the other side than it is to us. The citizens in Tel Aviv going about their normal daily work might be interested to know that Cairo Radio reported their city is burning.

"Tel Aviv is okay?" Ofra says, her face stunned as hope begins to beam.

"Shhh," Shlomo and the Pinskys hush her.

Until now, we've only heard reports from the Arab radios, gleefully announcing the death and destruction in our largest city, while the Israeli radio remained silent. This is the first real update on the situation of the war that we've heard since the air raid first wailed.

The general continues to speak. In a calm, British-accented Hebrew, he tells us that we must keep faith with our military and our government. *The fog of war obstructs the enemy, and so, let us leave him with it.*

Mrs. Friedburg nods. "I like this phrase, 'the fog of war,'" she says. "I told you we couldn't believe those first reports."

That night everyone falls asleep in the bomb shelter, some propped up against the wall, others curled on the grainy cement floor.

In the middle of the night, my sleep is suddenly shattered. The ground and air shake from the thunder of nearby mortar shells. It lasts for hours. Yoram whimpers and Esther moans, only half-awake but in the grips of a nightmare she can't shake. Ofra hushes them. She croons Persian lullabies to both the little children. I can barely hear her over the roar of war raging above us.

We keep a small light on, and it throws deep shadows in the corners. It's hard for me not to picture enemy soldiers crouching in those shadows.

The all-clear alarm never sounds.

At six in the morning, Shlomo turns on the radio. He had shut it off during the night to conserve batteries. After the rough night we just went through, we are braced for bad news. Kol Israel beeps in with a news update: *The lead story of the day is that yesterday the Air Force dealt a decisive blow to the air forces of the Egyptian, Syrian, and Jordanian armies. Four hundred enemy planes have been destroyed. The Chief of Staff described the victory as unprecedented.*

"Did you hear that?" gasps Ofra.

But the announcer signs off and music resumes.

"Can it be true?" my mom asks the room. "The Air Force destroyed four hundred planes?"

None of us can wrap our minds around that number. Three months ago, it was national news when our fighter planes downed *one* enemy aircraft in a dogfight. And here, in one day, four hundred? Is the Israeli Air Force making things up the same way our enemies did?

Mrs. Friedburg grins ear to ear.

"This report, I believe," she decrees.

We erupt in ragged cheers. Mrs. Friedburg hugs Shlomo. Ofra squeezes Esther and baby Yoram. My mom wraps me in her arms, and we rock from side to side in shocked joy. The elderly Mr. and Mrs. Pinsky start dancing.

Unprecedented is a mild word to describe this news. In one day, our little air force of two hundred planes has destroyed a force twice its size.

It's unbelievable. It's incredible. It's a miracle.

We are still stuck in our building's bomb shelter. The Jordanians are still shelling our city. But maybe the end of Israel isn't so near after all.

Chapter Thirteen
Day 2

We eat breakfast in the shelter. Though the radio news updates continue to tell us how well the war is going, the all-clear still hasn't sounded. We all agree, however, that the shelling has slowed.

"Ima," I say, "let me bring Beni home."

"No." She doesn't even stop to think about it. Baby Yoram is in her lap and she's tickling his belly. Yoram is a fat baby, and I always thought fat babies were happy, but he's very temperamental. He only lets Ofra or my mom hold him. When Mrs. Friedburg tried to feed him his bottle, he screamed and flailed his arms so hard he knocked the bottle out of her hands. It almost shattered on the hard floor. I think it hurt her feelings a little.

She handed the red-faced baby back to my mom and sniffed something under her breath about German babies having better manners.

"Beni should be here with us," I say.

"He's safer staying where he is."

Everyone knows it's safer to shelter in place. Even though Ofra badly needs to go to the hospital for her cut, we are waiting for the all-clear. The hospital is a kilometer away and hobbling there during shelling would be crazy.

"But Ima, he's probably losing his mind," I say. "You know how he gets when he's scared."

I picture Beni's rascally face scrunched in distress as he clutches his stomach. My mom clearly pictures the same thing. Her mouth twists in bitter worry as twin lines appear between her eyebrows. She shifts fat little Yoram on her lap, dislodging him from his perch on her chest.

"I can't let you," she says. "It's too dangerous."

Baby Yoram, annoyed that I'm encroaching on his turf and upsetting his cozy situation, grunts in irritation. His forehead wrinkles in ominous distress. My mom and I exchange alarmed looks. The last thing anyone wants is to set Yoram off. My mom jiggles him on her knees to distract him.

"I'll fly there so fast," I say urgently. "I can be at the school and back here with Beni in less than fifteen minutes. Please, Ima." I can't stand the thought of him in the school bunker with no family, with us so close. "I can bring Shira too," I offer to Ofra.

Ofra is lying down, her face flushed with fever. Little Esther is glued to her side.

"No," moans Ofra. "Just look at me! I don't want to scare her. Leave her at school."

"*I* should go get Beni," my mom says. As if he understands, baby Yoram whimpers and clings to her.

"They need you here," I say. "Plus, no offense, I'm much faster."

She snorts. I can't remember the last time I saw my mom run, even to catch a bus.

"I know you want to be a hero," she says softly. "But this isn't the way."

"Ima," I say, stung, "this isn't about that! Trust me. I just want to bring him back, I promise." And maybe it did cross my mind how heroic it would be to bring Beni home, but it is also true that he really would be better off here with us.

Mrs. Friedburg watches our conversation with great interest, her sharp, birdlike eyes following our back-and-forth like a soccer match.

"God." My mom puts a hand over her eyes. "I don't know. I don't want you to get hurt."

"There's hardly any shelling anymore," I argue. "We'll be fine. And Beni needs to be home with us."

"Let the boy go," Mrs. Friedburg butts in. For once I'm glad that she's nosy and in everyone's business.

"Really?" my mom asks her. She looks at the older woman, who, even after a night in our shelter, has her metal-gray hair in rigid curls and sits with perfect posture. Some sort of secret communication flies silently between them. I watch the two women, holding my breath.

Mrs. Friedburg nods firmly. She leans forward to pat my mom's hand in reassurance. "Bring your brother home," she says to me. "Fly back here on wings like an eagle's."

I know this quote. It's a line from Isaiah: *Those who hope in the Lord will renew their strength. They will fly up on wings like eagles'. They shall run and not be weary, they shall walk and not be faint.*

My mom bites her lip and looks down.

"Yes, Mrs. Friedburg," I say. My heart skips a beat knowing I'm going back out on the rubble-strewn street. "I will."

I plant a kiss on my mom's cheek, and she closes her eyes.

"Go," she says. "Bring Beni home. Come back safely."

* * *

The streets are empty as I leave the shelter and go outside. It's another lovely summer day. There's just the small matter of war raging. I take a moment to compose myself in my building's entryway. Then I take off, sprinting through the empty streets. The city feels abandoned. No shops open, no cars on the road. The breeze stirs a few pieces of laundry that still hang from their lines. A blue-and-white Israeli flag flaps from the top of a building. A sniper has shot holes through the Star of David in its center.

I make it all the way to Beni's school without incident. Easy-peasy, my racing heart notwithstanding.

Since it's my old school, I know right where to go. I bang on the door of the basement gymnasium until one of the teachers opens it. The familiar smell of old sweat and musty gym mats is now mixed with the body odor of too many people. Unlike the cheerful camaraderie in my building's shelter, the mood here is bleak and panicked.

"Did you hear the news?" I ask the teacher who lets me in. "About the Air Force?"

"No," she says. Her eyes are rimmed red from too little sleep. Dozens of small kids huddle in sad, frightened groups. "No one brought a radio. How bad is it?"

I don't recognize this teacher; she's a new lady. She's looks like an apple, with a huge chest and skinny legs. Her hair is stuffed into a messy emerald green snood, only making her more apple-like. She's clearly spent the night in her teaching clothes, and something that looks suspiciously like vomit stains the side of her long brown skirt.

"It's not bad news at all!" I can't believe that I am the one telling her this. My face glows with excitement. "We destroyed their air forces!"

"Whose?" she asks, confused. She's catching on that it's good news, but she hasn't absorbed the extent of it.

"Everyone's," I tell her. "Egypt. Jordan. Syria. Four hundred planes in one day!"

"What!" She clutches me by the upper arms, her long nails sinking into my skin. The sour smell of sweat and bad breath washes over me.

"It's true," I yelp. "Our air force caught them by surprise. Most of their planes were still on the ground."

"You're sure?" she asks, shaking me a bit.

"Yes!"

She loosens the painful grip on my arms, the pinched, frightened look slowly leaving her face.

"It was on the radio first thing this morning," I tell her. "That's why I came to get Beni. We're going to be fine! We're going to win!"

She squeals like a girl, then yanks me forward in a tight hug so that I sink into her massive bosom. I'm like a rag doll as she releases me. I catch a glimpse of her glowing, happy face as she plants two giant sloppy kisses on my cheeks.

She races off to tell the other teachers. I wade in, searching for my brother.

When I finally spot Beni, he is curled in on himself, rocking back and forth. Some of the older children are leading songs and games with the younger kids, but Beni isn't participating.

"Beni," I say. I put my hand on his curved back. He shakes under my hand like a field mouse, trembling with fear. "It's me, Motti. I'm here. Let's go home."

He raises a pale, tear-stained face.

"Motti." His eyes are almost blank with panic.

I feel nearly overwhelmed by the fear and need in his gaze. But I channel Mrs. Friedberg. I speak calmly, supremely confident.

"Enough partying at school. Ima's waiting. You ready to go home or what?"

His chin wobbles. "I miss Ima so much. I don't want to be here anymore."

"I know, Beni," I say. I punch him lightly on the shoulder and ruffle his hair. Anything to take away that lost, frightened look. "So let's scram."

A tiny hint of a smile lightens his face. Then he launches himself at me, burying his face in my chest and hugging me so tightly I gasp.

"I love you, Motti," he says, his voice muffled in my shirt.

"I love you too." My heart swells with a wave of affection for my little brother.

"I didn't know how long I would be here," he says, his words muffled against my shirt. "I'm so glad you came to get me. It feels like I've been here a year." His heart pounds so hard I can feel it thumping against my own chest. My heart answers his, beating loud and strong.

"I will always come get you," I promise him in that musty, smelly gymnasium. "You never have to worry about that."

* * *

We step out of the shelter, and Beni blinks in the bright sun.

"We can't dawdle," I say. "Take a deep breath, and then we've got to run. Understand?"

My little brother looks at me with his big, brown eyes. He slips his hand into mine and nods.

"Good. On three: one, two, three!"

We take off, running hand in hand. His school is a ten-minute walk from our building. I want to make it home in five minutes. We tear down the street, taking a left, then a right, running as if our lives depended on it.

"What are you doing outside?!" someone yells at us. I skid to a stop and see a Civil Defense man peering at us from a doorway.

"We're going home from school," I shout to him, standing in the middle of the road. No cars, after all. Beni heaves for breath next to me, making the most of the short rest.

"Get out from the middle of the road, stay close to the buildings!" the man yells back. "There are snipers out. Run, run, run!"

I don't bother to tell him the only reason we stopped was because he yelled a question at us.

"You ready?" I ask Beni. My brother nods,

and I squeeze his little hand. "We're almost there," I tell him.

We run and run, hugging the buildings, staying in the shadows. Past the bullet-riddled flag. Past the broken building with the cut laundry line. We're less than two minutes from our street.

A white cat crosses the street toward us. I skid to a stop on the sidewalk.

"What's wrong?" Beni gasps. His face is bright red, and he's gasping for breath. I've set a punishing pace for such a long sprint. He looks wildly all around us.

"It's the white cat," I say. "The one from yesterday." It seems like months ago that I saw it leap to the balcony and balance along the wrought iron edge like some kind of circus cat. But it happened only yesterday.

It comes right up to us, head cocked sideways to look at me.

"Oh," Beni says. "He's cute." The cat is pure white and small, even for a street cat. But he's graceful and light on his little padded feet.

"Yeah," I say, a smile coming out. "He is." His nose is a perfectly pink triangle. I feel a twinge of guilt that I ever tried to kick such a pretty cat. I think of Gideon and send a quick prayer that he's okay.

Beni and I crouch down. I put my hand out for the cat to sniff. The cat comes right up and rubs its little head against my hand, as if rubbing away an itch. Beni touches its tail and the cat flicks it out of his grasp, making Beni laugh.

Suddenly, it raises its head, hearing something neither Beni nor I can hear. Then it takes off without warning, streaking away and disappearing in the dark shade of a nearby alley.

"Where did he go?" Beni asks, squinting and half-turning to follow it.

"Doesn't matter," I say, though I'm suddenly uneasy. "We've stayed here too long, we need to go home."

We turn the corner and there's our building at the end of the street.

"Come on," I say. "Almost there."

At that very moment, a high-pitched whistle pierces the air. Without pausing to think, I grab my brother and shove us both against the sun-warmed building next to us. I press myself against Beni, covering his face with my arms.

A terrible roar explodes around us. The ground shakes. The power of the explosion shakes the eyeballs in my head. It rattles my bones. When silence falls again, I lift my head and look, checking Beni for cuts.

"Are you okay?" I ask. I can't hear myself speak. My ears are ringing.

Beni just stares at me with a dumbfounded look. I run my hands over his bare arms and legs, but he's okay. We're okay.

The shell landed near the end of the street. Blinking too fast, I step into the road to get a better look.

Our building is fine. I feel a wave of weakness at the intense relief. But something is different. For a moment I can't put my finger on it. Beni and I trot over to our building. I keep him a little bit behind me, my heart still tripping at the close call.

Then I finally realize what's different. The eucalyptus tree in our courtyard is gone. It's just . . . gone. Pulverized into matchsticks by a direct hit from a Jordanian shell. If we hadn't stopped to pet the snowy white cat, we would have been racing under that tree the moment it was hit.

"Wow," Beni breathes, looking at the destruction strewn all over the courtyard.

I start to shiver, shaking and jerking like a puppet being pulled by its strings. My hands look as if they belong to someone else. My knees feel loose and weak. A cat saved our lives.

Beni tugs me. "What are you waiting for?" he asks.

I realize that I've come to a complete stop, staring in shock at the giant scar where a huge tree stood a minute ago. Wisps of smoke and a campfire smell fill the air.

Beni doesn't understand how close we came to dying in the courtyard of our building.

"Motti," he complains, "you're squishing my fingers."

I pull myself together with difficulty and unclench the death grip I have on his small hand.

"It's okay," I croak. "We're almost home. Let's go."

Chapter Fourteen
Impossible Things

By the afternoon of the second day of the war, the all-clear siren blares. No more mortar shells drop on Jerusalem. No more snipers shoot into the streets of our city. We move out of the basement shelter and back into our apartment.

Shlomo and Mrs. Friedburg make the long walk with Ofra to the hospital while my mom stays home with Yoram, Esther, Shira, Beni, and me. Ofra returns late that night with twenty stiches under a thick wrapping of white gauze. She's pale and haggard with fatigue. I hang back in the doorway of my room, listening in on their conversation. Beni's soft, steady breaths tell me he's asleep. Shira and Esther are in Gideon's room. Yoram sleeps in a little nest made of blankets next to our couch.

"How was it?" my mom asks, after hugging her.

"It was terrible." Ofra's head droops in fatigue. Dark circles add the only color on her pale face. "So crowded."

"Wounded soldiers?" my mom asks.

"Yes, and so many civilians. The nurses were running around deciding who would get painkillers and who didn't need them so much."

"They're worried they'll run out?"

Ofra nods. "They think thousands more might be coming."

"God forbid," my mom says, a hand to her mouth.

"I should take the children back upstairs," Ofra says wearily.

"Are you crazy? They're all asleep." My mom turns Ofra and shoos her out. "They'll be fine here. Go rest. I'll see you in the morning."

After Ofra leaves, my mom gently picks up Yoram and buries her nose in the crook of his little neck. I crawl back into bed.

At some point in the night, Shira must have kicked Esther in her sleep. All I know is there's a loud thump and then Esther wails loudly, waking everyone. It takes a long time before my mom can settle her down again and she falls asleep.

All night I hear artillery shells booming in the distance. We're out of the bomb shelter, but the war is still raging on.

* * *

We spend the next morning playing pick-up sticks and card games, too unnerved by the past two days to play outside. The light that pours into our living room is bright and harsh. All my life, the morning sunlight streamed into the house in dappled circles, shaded through the branches of the eucalyptus tree. Now there's no shade. No tree. It makes being in my own home feel weird and different. It's hotter in the living room now. And exposed. I can see straight through to the building across the courtyard, and the windows in those apartments stare right back at us. It's even worse in Shira's apartment.

Their west-facing flat has no glass in the windows.

All morning I've had a restless feeling. I assume it's because I'm stuck inside with too many kids in the apartment. There's a pressure inside my chest that keeps me from sitting still. I shift and turn, trying to get the tightness to loosen.

We're all in the living room, sprawled on the cool tile floor reading and coloring, when the music playing on the radio is interrupted by an urgent update. Everyone falls silent, even Esther and the baby.

This report just in: Colonel Motta Gur, commander of a reserve paratroop brigade, has just announced: "The Temple Mount is in our hands."

My mom screams. Shira and I freeze, not sure we understand what's happening.

"What's wrong?" Beni cries. We spent yesterday and the day before in a bomb shelter. Hearing my mom screaming at news from the radio is scary.

"Children," my mom says, her voice wobbling, her face flushed, her eyes rimmed with tears. “Do you understand? The Western Wall! The Old City! It’s ours again!”

She grabs Beni and smothers him into her bosom. Shira and I exchange wide-eyed, open-mouthed looks.

There’s a rap on the door, and before we can open it, the Pinskys from upstairs spill into our apartment.

“Did you hear? Did you hear the news?” Efraim Pinsky shouts, his wrinkled face shining.

“Yes!” my mom says, gasping with happiness. “I can’t believe it!”

“I am seventy-three years old,” he says. “When I lost my parents and five siblings in the Holocaust I thought that God had abandoned me and the Jewish people. Now I know that God has blessed me. For me to see this day!” He raises hands dotted with age spots to the ceiling. “God has not forgotten the Jewish people!”

Mrs. Friedberg and Shlomo and Ofra enter through the open door.

“Did you hear?” they cry.

The next thing I know, all of us except Ofra are somehow holding hands in a big circle.

Me, Beni, Shira, Esther, my mom, Efraim and Miriam Pinsky, Shlomo and Mrs. Friedburg, and we're dancing the *hora* in my living room, singing "*Hevenu Shalom Aleichem*" and laughing like crazy. The same people who huddled in the bomb shelter the day before. We're dancing.

Efraim, his wispy white hair standing on end, kisses my mom, a big juicy kiss right on her lips. He lets her go, and before I can do anything, he plants one on me. I stagger back, and then Beni gets kissed. I start laughing hysterically at the look of horror on my brother's face. Mrs. Friedburg has her hands up like she's going to stop Efraim from kissing her next, but he dodges the halfhearted effort, wraps his hands around her face, and kisses her long and hard.

Happiness spills out from everyone in a different way. Miriam Pinsky is doing some dance move from the 1920s, as little Esther tries to mimic her steps. Shlomo cuts in, and they start doing a soft shuffle by the bookcase, dancing cheek to cheek. Ofra sits on the couch, her bandaged leg propped up, and wipes tears of happiness from her face.

Shira holds baby Yoram and our eyes meet. In the happy chaos, for one tiny moment, all the noise falls away. There is such pure joy shining in her big, brown eyes. The crazy grin on my face eases into something more normal. A happy smile. It feels like there's only Shira and me and a beautiful world where prayers are answered and amazing things, impossible things, can happen.

My mom breaks out the good brandy and the adults all toast each other, then the paratroopers, Colonel Motta Gur, Defense Minister Moshe Dayan, pretty much anyone they can think of. They laugh and hug, unable to wrap their minds all the way around the fact that the impossible has actually come true.

* * *

Eventually the Pinskys go back to their apartment. Ofra hobbles upstairs to rest. Mrs. Friedburg announces she's going for a walk. And it's back to being us five kids alone in the apartment with my mom.

Yoram, too keyed up from a bad night's sleep and all the excitement, screams instead of napping. There's nowhere in the apartment to get away from his ear-piercing shrieks. He hates the pallet my mom made for him from blankets and pillows. He wants his bed. But she can't take him upstairs to his mom yet. Ofra needs quiet and rest.

"Go outside," my mom commands us. "You're keeping him awake."

Little Esther stays, but Beni, Shira, and I head out.

There are cars on the road, people in the street. Yesterday's eerie silence is gone. The corner market has reopened and shoppers are inside, stocking up on groceries. Everything is back to normal. Although we all know it's not. Not really. The Old City might be ours, but the war isn't over. Our soldiers are still fighting, and if they lose ground, if the momentum turns, then we'll be under fire again. Buildings will be blown up. More people will be hurt. The radio had said nearly a thousand civilians in Jerusalem have been injured in the shelling of the past two days.

The three of us enter the corner store. The familiar smells of newsprint, cardamom, and coffee greet us. The wire racks that hold the morning edition of the local papers are nearly empty. Everyone's been buying a copy, wanting to know what's going on. There are newspapers in Hebrew, Yiddish, English, and several other languages that I don't even recognize. Shoppers chat excitedly about the news report. It's clear our lives will change after this war is over.

The owner of the shop eyes us as we enter, but he's too busy with a line of customers to hassle us for hanging out in his store. Besides, it's not a normal day. He stands behind a glass counter that usually holds pastries and snacks. But the bakery isn't up to full speed and the only thing he has to sell is bread.

A transistor radio mounted on a high corner shelf beeps with a news update. Everyone in the store falls silent as the latest report from the front lines comes on. In addition to repeating Motta Gur's pronouncement about the Temple Mount, the announcer mentions that information is still coming in from a fierce battle in the Old City that took place late last night. A place called Ammunition Hill. Another battle near the YMCA was nicknamed "The Alley of Death" by the soldiers who survived it. Only half the original force managed to cross five hundred meters.

I shiver at the thought of it.

Shira and I exchange glances. Ammunition Hill is only a few kilometers away from us. It's high ground among the seven hills that ring Jerusalem. It got its name in the First World War, since it's where the British stored a lot of their ammunition. It's been an important military position first for the British, then for the Jordanians. It's riddled with mines, trenches, and bunkers. The thought of shells hitting people the way they hit my tree twists inside me. Oh, Gideon. Please don't be hurt.

Shira has a few coins in her pocket, and she buys three pieces of Bazooka gum that she shares with Beni and me. The bright pink gum fills my mouth with delicious sugar. Everything is normal. Sort of. We read the jokes inside the wrappers, but they aren't very funny.

As we leave the shop, I see Moishe across the street.

He's carrying something, and we jog over to see what he's got.

"Check this out," he says. He holds up the black metal tail fin from a Jordanian mortar shell. It looks like part of a satellite or a rocket. I am instantly jealous. This is the neatest thing I've ever seen.

"Where did you get that?" I demand. "How come it isn't in bits and pieces?"

Moishe grins at my reaction.

"Duds," he says. "Some of the shells land funny and the tail pops off. Sometimes the tail survives a live round too."

"Where did you find it?" I ask again. Maybe there are more. I can already picture one on the small shelf above my bed. Or if I found two, I could build a little stepping bench with tail fins for legs.

"That building that was hit on Rodef Street. The tail was just lying there, near some of the stones."

Beni and I exchange looks. We passed that

building yesterday, not far from the white cat. If only I had thought to stop and look for tail fins instead of petting a cat!

I don't even ask if Moishe would trade for it. I know that I have to find my own tail fin.

"Did you hear?" he says. "School starts back up tomorrow."

We groan a bit, and then he leaves to show off the tail to David and Avi, who just stepped out of another shop. I see the small huddle that forms around him. Everyone's going to be on the hunt for those things.

"Come on," Shira says. Her eyes are twinkling like mine. "There're other places that were hit. I passed one on the way home from school yesterday."

Shira's all-girls school is in the opposite direction from mine and Beni's, so I haven't been that way since before the shelling.

"Let's go," I say.

"I don't want to," Beni says, in a near whine.

"Don't be a baby," I say, irritated. "We have to go now, or someone else will find all the tail fins. And then we'll miss our chance forever."

"I don't want to."

"So go home!" I say. "If you're such a baby, then you should just nap with Yoram and Esther."

Beni draws himself up to his full height.

"I am not a baby."

"So come with us." I suddenly realize I have to get him to come. If Beni goes home and tells my mom we're digging around the rubble for dud shells, it won't go over well. "Come on," I wheedle. "Let's check it out. Who knows what we'll find."

Beni scowls at the ground. I've hurt his feelings, and he's digging in his heels.

Shira watches us and, seeing that my charm and powers of persuasion aren't working, comes up with a better solution.

"I'll buy you another piece of Bazooka," she offers.

Beni considers the bribe.

"Two pieces," he says, his eyes narrowed.

Shira sighs. "Fine. Two pieces."

"Deal!"

"But *after* we look for the tail fins," I hurry to add. Not that Beni is a weasel, but it'll be safer to pay the bribe after he does what he says he'll do, not before. I've pulled off that little trick too many times to fall for it myself.

He looks like he wants to argue, but I cut him off. "Time's wasting. Other people are looking for tails too. And school starts tomorrow, so we go now and you get your prize after."

"Okay," he says. "But you have to promise you'll really buy me two pieces."

"I promise," Shira says. She looks at me, as if trying to tell me something, but I can't read her gaze. I hope she really does have the extra money for two pieces.

The three of us head off to the bombed-out building.

The restless, uneasy feeling from this morning is back. It feels like a strange itch or a pinch. I'm twitchy and I can't settle. Even though I got my way and we're off to look for tail fins, I can't shake the feeling that something is wrong.

The news report about Ammunition Hill particularly bothers me, though I've had this unhappy feeling even before I heard the news.

The thought of people fighting and dying so close to where I live makes me feel sick.

I glance uneasily over my shoulder as we walk. I can't put my finger on it. I check Shira and Beni with a sideways glance, but they seem fine. Beni chatters about a magic trick with a cup and a stick that one of the teachers in the shelter showed him. Shira smiles and nods. Maybe I look normal on the outside too.

When we get to the building, there are a few Civil Defense men organizing a cleanup crew. There's no way we can poke around the crumbled stones and concrete.

"Let's go around the back," Shira says. "They won't be able to see us in the alley."

"Good idea," I say.

There isn't much rubble in the shadow-dark alley. The blast hit the front of the building and scattered it into the street.

The alley reeks of urine and rotting trash. The garbage men are busy fighting a war. The cobblestones are slick from where someone dumped a bucket of soapy wash water. Dirty soap bubbles have settled in the edges of the worn stones. “This is stupid,” I say after a while. “We need to look somewhere wide and open where shells would land without hitting anything. That’s where the duds are going to be, not in the alley.”

“Don’t give up so quickly,” Shira says, picking her way around an overflowing metal dumpster. “A shell hit the front of the building, so maybe something landed back here too.”

“It stinks,” Beni whines. The old trash has meat in it, and the smell of rot hangs heavy in the air.

“Yes, we’ve all noticed,” I say, annoyed.

The unhappy feeling inside me grows. I feel like my skin is too tight.

Then Beni moans and grabs my arm.

“Motti,” he says. “Look!”

Chapter Fifteen
Too Late

A glimpse of white fur catches my eye.

It's the snow-white cat from the day before. It's on its side, half under a dumpster, its legs sprawled in a graceless tangle. Even in the dim shadow of the alley, its fur gleams. The sight of it lances me with pain.

"Don't go near it," I say, grabbing Beni's upper arm, holding him back.

Shira looks at me and at Beni, not understanding why we're so upset.

"Don't let Beni near, okay?" I tell her.

"Sure," she says. She has younger siblings, so she knows how to take charge. "Here, Beni." She digs into her pocket. "Why don't you hold the money for your gum?" She hands Beni a half-lira coin that he eagerly reaches for.

I really don't want to take a closer look, but maybe the cat is only injured and we can help. Maybe it's a different cat. I swallow thickly. It looks deflated. Like a puppet without a hand inside to make it move.

As I approach, I know that it's too late. I crouch to get a better look. It's the same cat. Pure white and small. Its eyes are slightly open and dull, its chest totally still. I can see now that it was hurt, probably by falling debris. It must have staggered here, hoping to hide while it recovered. But instead it died, all alone in a smelly back alley.

It's a stupid stray cat, I tell myself, fiercely blinking back tears. *It doesn't matter what happens to it.* But even as I lie to myself, I know it's not true. This cat was beautiful and funny. It saved me and Beni. If something as perfect as this cat can get smashed, then nothing and no one is safe.

Shira and Beni watch me as I rise to my feet. I shake my head.

"There's nothing we can do," I say, still looking down at the cat. "It's already dead."

"We just saw it yesterday," Beni says, almost confused at how something could go from alive to dead so quickly. "We should have brought it inside the bomb shelter."

He's right, we should have.

"The adults would never have let you bring it inside," Shira points out. "You know how they are about stray cats."

It's true. My mom always hisses when she sees a cat, shooing it away.

"Should we bury it?" Beni asks in a small voice.

"Yes," Shira says simply. "We should."

I don't know any other girl who would be so calm and helpful right now. She doesn't ask why we're upset, why we care about this cat. Our eyes meet. I am so full of words and feelings that nothing comes out. But Shira seems to understand.

"It was a really pretty cat," she says.

"This cat saved our lives," I finally say. "When I brought Beni back from school." I tell her how petting the cat kept us away from the courtyard when the shell hit the tree.

"Oh," Shira says. She blinks rapidly.

I don't tell her how I tried to kick the cat last month or that Gideon was the one who stopped me.

We find an empty cardboard box and tip the little body into it. We carry it home, taking turns holding the box. It's a strange funeral procession.

A few neighbors have already started cleaning up the mess from the blown-up tree in the courtyard. It's easy to borrow a shovel and find a quiet corner to dig a small grave. A light breeze kicks up as I dig, cooling my sweat, bringing with it the smell of cedar and smoke. A tumble of silver-green eucalyptus leaves, remains of the tree, scatter in the light gusts.

Shira dashes to her apartment and returns with a clean nappy. We tip the cat out of the cardboard box onto the square white cloth. Shira rolls it into a shroud. We each grab an end and lay the small bundle in the hole I've made. We stand above the hole, looking at the small thing inside.

"Well," Beni says, "good-bye, cat. Thank you for helping us yesterday. We will never forget you."

My six-year-old brother has said everything there is to say.

"Amen," I whisper.

Shira nods. "Rest in peace."

I scoop from the mound of dirt next to the hole and shovel it all back in.

My mom steps out on the balcony.

"Motti, Beni, Shira!" she calls out. "Lunchtime!"

Other parents have stepped out on their balconies, calling their children inside. It's something they usually do in the evening, calling us back in after a whole afternoon of playing.

"Coming!" I shout back.

We head back into the apartment. I wonder if the bad feeling I've had all day was because I somehow knew the cat had been hurt and had died. Now that I know it's dead, I expect that feeling to fade—the way that worry about an upcoming test goes away as soon as I take the test. Even before the grade comes back, the fear of the test itself is gone.

But as we jog up the dim stairwell, our eyes adjusting to the gloom after the bright sun outside, that heavy feeling in my chest hasn't left me.

I worry about my dad and my brother. I worry about us. The snow-white cat's fate only heightens my fear.

After all, anything can happen. Impossible things.

Chapter Sixteen
Gideon

The next day, the fourth day of the war, Beni and I return to school. I'm glad to be back.

"Your education comes first," my parents always say. The Jews have a long history of being kicked out of the countries they lived in, so we have always revered learning as the one form of wealth that can never be stolen. Because while tools, money, and land can be taken away, knowledge cannot. So it doesn't surprise me that school reopens the moment it's deemed safe. No one, especially not our enemies, will keep us from learning.

It feels good to be busy and to pretend that everything is normal.

That afternoon my dad gets a few hours of leave. He's stationed a few kilometers away from the front with the quartermaster unit. He hasn't seen any fighting. Now that all the fighting has been pushed out of Israel and into the other countries, we feel much safer.

More rumors trickle in about the terrible battle at Ammunition Hill. It might end up being one of the worst battles in this war, with hundreds of dead on both the Jordanian and Israeli sides. I can't shake my fear about Gideon, but when we see my dad, he reassures us.

He saw Gideon come through his base on the first day of the war. They managed to snatch a brief conversation. He doesn't think Gideon's unit had been assigned to go to the hill.

"I'm sure he's fine," my dad tells my mom. He's sunburned and tired, with purple shadows under his eyes. "You should have seen him," he says, his lips crooking in a smile. "He looked great. The whole unit was cracking jokes. They're fine."

My mom has had a furrow between her eyebrows for days now. It eases for a moment at my father's calm confidence.

"I just wish we could hear from Gideon," my mom says, not swept away by the wave of growing euphoria sweeping our city. "I heard that the Kellermans already had a letter from their son."

"You worry too much," my dad says, patting her back comfortingly. "He's too busy to write us right now. That's normal. Our boys have pushed the fight so far into Jordan and Egypt that the generals are arguing about how far to go!" My dad's eyes sparkle with elation. "I'm telling you, this war might end up being the best thing that ever happened to our country. The Old City is ours!" He shakes his head in wonder. "Two hundred years from now the Jewish people will celebrate this as a greater miracle than Hanukkah and Purim combined!"

It's almost unreal to hear that coming from my dad after the month of fear and stress that led up to the war. But he's right that the news reports coming in are all amazingly, almost miraculously in our favor. Our military pushed the Egyptians literally into the Suez Canal. In Jordan, our forces drove the Jordanians out of the Old City and the West Bank.

"Jerusalem is ours," my dad repeats, his face flushed red with sunburn and excitement. "After two thousand years. Did you ever think you'd live to see this day?"

He turns to smile at me. "After the fighting is over, I'll take you there. I'll show you my old house, my neighborhood streets. There's no place on earth like the alleyways of the Old City." I can see it: the five of us wandering through the streets, my dad pointing out his childhood hangouts.

My dad returns to the base after a quick meal with us. He promises to try and see us again soon.

* * *

The next day is Saturday. The house is quiet. Ofra is mobile enough to take care of her children now. Our apartment has been blessedly free of Geffens since yesterday afternoon. I try to read *All Quiet on the Western Front.* It's told from the point of view of a nineteen-year-old soldier who thinks that war will be a great adventure, but instead everything is terrible. One by one his friends are killed. Plus, there's nothing to eat. After a while I put the book down. I never did manage to get it to Gideon. Maybe I did him a favor.

We stay close to the radio, listening to updates about the fifth day of the war. The war is clearly winding down. There's talk in the international community about a cease-fire. The Arab countries are starting to sound interested in declaring an end to the fighting. But until my dad and Gideon are home safe, we can't rest.

My mom is filled with a nervous energy. Since the Geffen children returned home, she's been scrubbing floors, vacuuming rugs, dusting, and baking elaborate desserts from morning to night. It's as if she was trying to dirty as many dishes as possible so she had more to clean. I think she was glad to have all those extra kids to keep her busy. But now that it's Shabbat, she can't do chores to keep herself busy. She just paces restlessly and keeps ducking out of the apartment to talk to our neighbors.

By the time I give up on my book, my mom is setting out a platter of cinnamon-sugar *rugalah* that she baked yesterday. I reach for a cookie.

"Only one," my mom says. "The rest are for the Geffens. Ofra's stitches are inflamed and she has to go back to the clinic. The kids are coming down here in a few minutes." She almost sounds happy at the thought of chaos entering our apartment again.

"Will they spend the night?" I ask. I wouldn't mind having Shira's company.

"I don't know yet," she says, setting the platter down in the center of the coffee table. "It depends on what the nurse says. If the leg is very bad, they might keep her overnight. Otherwise, they'll just give her penicillin."

When I hear steps in the hallway outside our door, I assume that the Geffen children are tromping down from upstairs. I slip a cookie in my pocket. Cookies don't tend to last long around guests. A moment later, we hear a firm series of knocks.

That's not how kids knock.

I suddenly feel a wave of goose bumps shiver down my back. The hair on the back of my neck rises.

"Ima," I say in a strangled voice. "Don't answer that."

At the same time Beni comes out of his room rubbing his eyes, still wearing my old green truck pajamas. After lunch my mom insisted he take a nap, though he complained to high heaven that he didn't need one.

"I fell asleep," Beni grumbles accusingly. "What's going on?"

"Don't open it!" I say at the same time that my mom pulls open the door.

Two men in Class A olive-green uniforms stand in the hall. My skin prickles hot and cold. There is only one reason the army sends two soldiers in Class A's to a family's home.

My mom just stands there, frozen.

I stare at the young soldiers, my heart thumping in my chest as if I'm teetering on the edge of a cliff. A dark pit yawns below me.

"Oh, no." My mom raises a shaking hand to her lips. "No. Please."

"I'm very sorry," says one soldier. He looks miserable. He holds some papers in his hand. "May I come inside?"

"No." My mom shakes her head. "No!"

"What is it?" Beni cries, looking in confusion from the soldiers to my mom and me. "What's wrong?"

"I'm so sorry," says the first guy. "I'm here to tell you that Private Gideon Laor has fallen."

"No!" my mom shrieks, covering her ears. Her scream rips into me. It's the sound of pure horror and grief. "I don't want you here! Go away!"

She starts to close the door, and the soldier puts his hand out to stop her. Beni, crying without even full understanding, runs to my mom.

"Go away!" he yells at the soldiers, standing in front of my mom as if he could protect her. "Leave my mom alone!"

She covers her ears, shaking her head "no" as if she can stop the news from reaching her, as if she can stop it from happening. Beni tries to wrap his arms around her, but she's so far gone, she doesn't even realize he's there.

Even as part of me knows it isn't their fault, I hate the soldiers. We were fine, we were okay, until they showed up with their terrible, earth-cracking news.

Across the hallway, Mrs. Friedburg opens her door. She takes in the scene, understanding the situation in an instant. She looks at me, her face suddenly haggard and old. She hurries past the soldiers, rushing upstairs.

"I'll take those papers," I say numbly, walking to the doorway and reaching for them. The soldiers exchange looks. The first soldier hands them to me.

"Can we come in?" the soldier repeats uncomfortably. "We usually sit and stay with the family until friends arrive. It's not good to be alone with news like this."

"No," my mom says woodenly. Her arms are wrapped around Beni in an automatic gesture of comfort. "Go away."

"We can't stay if you don't want us," the soldier says, looking exhausted. "It's your choice. But we're here for you."

"Ima, it's okay," I hear Beni tell my mom. "They're leaving. It's okay, Ima."

My mom's legs give out from under her and she sinks down to the ground, taking Beni with her. She's still shaking her head, as if by disagreeing with the news she can change it.

Then we hear Mrs. Friedburg and Ofra making their way slowly down the stairs. Ofra leans on Mrs. Friedburg's shoulder, her leg bandaged and tender. But infected leg or not, she's here ready to help.

"We've got it," Mrs. Friedburg says to the young soldiers, her German accent thicker than usual. "You boys go. We'll handle this."

"Okay." The soldier nods in relief. "Thank you."

"Do you know what happened to him?" I ask, breaking through the numbness.

"He—he died," one of them says awkwardly.

"No," I shake my head. "I mean, where? How did it happen?"

"We don't know too much yet," the other one says. He's short with wiry, curly hair. "His unit is the one that was caught in the Alley of Death."

The Alley of Death. I close my eyes and all I see is Gideon.

The curly-haired soldier crouches down so that we're eye to eye. "This war has cost us a lot," he says in a low voice. "There isn't a family in Jerusalem that hasn't suffered." He isn't much older than Gideon. There's a sadness in his face that seems ancient. "It's only because your brother was strong and brave that we're safe. That's a terrible price for your family to pay. But truly, your brother died so that our country could go on." I stare at his polished black combat boots. There's a small scuff on the right boot. It makes him suddenly human. I can't hate someone with scuffed boots.

"When we stand before God and give an account of our lives," he continues in a low voice, "we have to say what we did, who we helped, how we shaped the world and made it better. Your brother will be able to say: 'I saved my country, I unified Jerusalem, I protected my family.'" I look at him, stone-faced. He meets my eyes. He swallows heavily. "There aren't many people who can say that."

I don't care about accounting before God. As far as I'm concerned, God has a lot of accounting to do before me.

"How many families have you visited today?" I ask.

The soldier shakes his head. “Too many.” He sighs. “You’re not suffering alone.” He squeezes my shoulders, as if to press in strength. Then he rises to his full height.

As we speak, Mrs. Friedburg and Ofra lift my mom off the floor and guide her onto the couch. They sit Beni down and make him a cup of chocolate milk. They pour my mom a shot of brandy and force her to drink it. Their low, soothing murmurs calm the air. The platter of cookies sits on the low coffee table as if we’ve been expecting guests. As if my mom made food for the mourners instead of the other way around.

“I’m deeply sorry,” the first soldier says.

“You should go,” I say.

The soldier nods, accepting my order. He extends his hand and automatically I take it. “Gideon was a great guy and a brave soldier.” He shakes my hand firmly. Then both men salute me. “The country will never forget his service, and the sacrifice he made so that we may live.”

I stare at the soldiers. They’re saluting me like I’ve done something good, but I haven’t done anything. None of this feels real to me. I wonder if I will wake up in my bed. Maybe none of this is real.

They leave, disappearing down the stairs.

I remain rooted in my spot by the door. I watch the scene inside my apartment as if I'm looking at someone else's family, someone else's story, someone else's loss. Mrs. Friedburg has placed a mug of something warm in my mom's limp hands. Ofra has pulled Beni into her lap, rocking and murmuring to him.

Gideon, gone? I shake my head as if to banish the thought. Gideon, who is strong and agile and can race across the top of a chain-link fence, has *fallen*? The thought sends a shard of pain so deep into my heart that I gasp. I'm losing my balance; I'm going to fall into that black pit. What are the Three Musketeers without their best, strongest partner?

I suddenly can't bear it. I can't stand to be in the apartment. I slip away through the open door, feeling like I'm going to be sick. Gideon, gone?

The world has stopped making sense. I'm falling.

Chapter Seventeen
Explosion

I don't know where to go, what to do. My feet take me to the back alley behind our street. I sink down, elbows against my knees, leaning my face against my hands. I sit like that for a long time, not really thinking about anything. I don't know how much time passes before I hear a little sound, something brushing against a pile of newspapers fluttering under a rock. I slowly raise my head.

Yellow eyes stare at me. A spotted black and brown cat crouches near me. It flicks a white tufted ear. It has a scar across its face and its tail is short, as if it has been pinched off. This is a battle-hardened cat, not nearly as beautiful as the snow-white cat. Maybe only the toughest survive. It twitches its pink little nose. I stay as still as possible, barely breathing.

Deciding that I seem harmless, it gracefully sits and lifts a paw. It licks and licks and licks, turning its little paw this way and that. I don't know why I'm so fascinated, but I can't seem to look away. I realize that the cat is tending to a cut. It hasn't sailed through the war so easily after all.

I dig through my pocket and pull out the crumbly *rugalah.* The smell of cinnamon turns my stomach. I can't imagine eating again.

"Here," I say. My voice is hoarse, as if I've been shouting.

The cat flinches at the sound. It stops licking and tenses, braced to flee.

"I'm not going to hurt you," I say softly. "Eat this." I place the *rugalah* halfway between us. Do cats even eat cookies?

The cat puts down its wounded paw. It looks at the cookie, then at me, then the cookie. It's clearly hungry. But it doesn't trust me.

I push myself away, scooting down the wall so I sit a bit farther back.

"I'm not going to hurt you," I tell it again. My voice is raspy and hoarse. "The food is all yours."

After a long pause, the cat daintily takes two steps and sits in front of the cookie. Its green eyes flick to me once more, and then it quickly snatches it and runs off with its prize, limping slightly.

I sigh—happy that the cat took the food, sad that it didn't trust me enough to eat it next to me.

"Motti! Motti?"

I blink, and the cat is gone.

Shira's calling. She comes around the corner of the building and stops when she sees me. My heart squeezes at the look on her face. She knows about Gideon. For one small moment with the cat, I had managed to forget. The realization that he's never coming home hits me all over again. This is something terrible that will never be undone.

"Everyone's looking for you," she says. "Your dad's on his way home. We called the base."

I shake my head.

"Motti, I'm so sorry."

I shake my head again. If I try to speak, then I'll just cry.

"You don't want to go home?" she asks softly.

I shrug.

"Okay." She nods as if I've clearly explained myself. "We don't have to go right away."

I push myself to my feet.

"Let's go to the stadium." My voice is rough and growly. She blinks in surprise. It's not that I want to play soccer, but I can't think of anywhere else to go.

We walk in silence. I feel her looking at me with every step, but she lets the silence stay, which I'm deeply grateful for. I really don't want to talk about it. As we approach the field, I see my friends. But they're not playing soccer. They stand in a huddle, pointing and looking at something lying on the end of our field.

I trot over to my friends. Shira hangs back. She is always shy around the rowdy boys I hang out with.

"What is it?" I ask, coming up to the group.

It feels so normal. My friends are laughing and joking. They can't tell anything is wrong.

I can't believe that so much sadness and shock doesn't show on my face or in the very color of my skin.

"Moishe found a shell," Avi says with glee.

Another tail fin for Moishe. I feel a faint echo of jealousy.

"Lucky," I say, trying to think of what normal people say in situations like this. "That's his second tail fin." Somewhere in the back of my mind, I remember wanting one so badly only a couple of days ago.

"It's the whole shell. It never exploded."

"Wait, what?" I focus where Avi's pointing.

He's right. It isn't just a tail fin—it's the entire mortar shell, half-buried in the grassy dirt. It's as long as my arm, with a bright green shell and yellow Arabic writing. The black finned tail sticks up.

Moishe bends down and scoops up a few rocks.

"Watch this, guys," he says. He whips his arm back and throws the rock. It pings off the shell.

"What are you doing?" I say. The numbness around me starts to crack. Everyone knows you don't mess with unexploded mortars. There are posters at school that warn people to stay away and call the police if they find anything. "Stop!"

Moishe looks at me like I'm crazy. "What are you worried about? It's a dud. It's not going to blow." He throws another rock and misses.

"Don't be a moron," I say. "You've got to stop."

"Motti!" Shira comes jogging toward us. I don't want her to tell everyone about Gideon. As soon as everyone else knows, it will be real. "We should go back," she says, looking uneasy.

"Brave Motti," Moishe taunts. "What happened? A few days in the bunker turned you into a crybaby? Are you going to run off with your girlfriend?"

"No," I say hotly. "You're acting like an idiot." I realize suddenly that I sound like Gideon. The thought chokes me into silence. Shira reaches us.

"Oh, yeah?" Moishe says. "Can an idiot make this shot?"

"Motti," Shira says, putting a hand on my arm. "We should go back."

"Don't!" I yell at Moishe. Shira's standing between me and him. I can't stop it.

"Watch this!" Moishe spins and whips his arm. A rock the size of a tangerine flies out of his hand. It sails in a low arch. My breath catches in my throat. It nails the half-buried shell. I hear a loud metallic *chink*.

A split-second later, there's a tremendous boom that almost knocks us down.

Everyone covers their heads. We're showered with dirt and stones. A few kids drop to the ground, curling in on themselves the way we practice in school in case we're stuck outside in an air raid. Two kids scream in terror. I can see their mouths open, but for a few seconds I can't hear anything except the ringing in my ears.

I scan everyone to make sure we're all okay.

"Anyone hurt?" I shout. My hearing slowly returns.

My friends get to their feet, looking pale and dazed. The dirt is raw and ripped in a small crater around where the mortar used to lie. We're incredibly lucky. The mortar broke apart into several large chunks that missed us as they flew by.

"Moishe, you're an idiot!" Shira yells and smacks Moishe's arm. There's dirt in her hair and on her clothes.

"No one got hurt, right?" he says defensively. He rubs his arm. Shira left a red mark. "That's what matters."

"We have to get out of here," Miki says, his eyes too wide. "Civil Defense will come to see what the explosion was about. Let's go!"

He's right. We're going to be in so much trouble. Boys drift away, eager to disappear. I turn to follow.

"Motti, Motti," Shira says, pulling on my arm. I shake her off. I don't want to talk about Gideon. "Motti!" She tugs on my arm hard enough to stop me in my tracks. "Look at David."

David stands still, like a statue, fifty feet from us. There are clumps of grass in his hair and his arms are covered in a fine dusting of dirt, but he hasn't moved to brush himself off. In fact, he stands unnaturally still. I don't think he even ducked when the shell blew.

"David!" I shout to him. "What are you doing? Let's get out of here!"

The police could be here any minute. We need to be gone.

He stares at me, so I know he heard me. But he doesn't move.

"What's wrong with him?" I ask Shira. But she's gone stiff. The streaks of dirt on her face are stark against her suddenly pale skin.

"Look," she says in a small, tight voice. "Look what he's holding."

Tucked under his arm, like a rolled up newspaper, is another bright yellow mortar. The black metal tail is like a starburst next to his chest.

Chapter Eighteen
Hero

"Put it down!" I shout at him. "What are you waiting for? Just put it DOWN!"

David won't move. His eyes meet mine, pleading for help, but his legs are frozen in place. His chest heaves as if he can't get enough air. He must have picked it up before Moishe blew up the other shell. He probably thought he would take it home as a souvenir. Now that he knows it could be live, he's scared to move in case it blows. The smallest nudge could jog the trigger wire into place. I can't let myself think about what that mortar could do to him.

"Shira," I say, breathing heavily. "Go get help. Quickly."

I have never been so afraid in my life. My legs have gone leaden with fear. My arms are heavy at my sides. My throat is instantly parched. I can barely swallow.

Without wasting a second, Shira turns on her heels, flying like the wind toward our neighborhood. David and I are now alone in the field. Where are the Civil Defense men when you need them?

"It's okay," I croak. The words nearly strangle in my throat. I lick my lips and try again. "It's okay, David." I know that Gideon wouldn't have been this scared if he were here instead of me. I know that the famous spy Eli Cohen was never this scared. I know that I'm not really a hero.

But I also know that I will not leave my friend alone in the field, holding a live mortar.

My legs disagree with me. They don't want to move.

I concentrate with all my might and manage to take one shaking step toward David.

"Don't worry," I say, not taking my eyes off David. I imagine that Gideon is walking next to me. I picture his sturdy frame and loping stride at my side. I take another step closer to my friend. "See how I'm walking? We can do this. We'll do it together."

David's eyes cling to me. As I draw closer, I see that his face is shiny with sweat, his legs trembling from the strain of staying absolutely still.

"It's not a grenade," I say. "It doesn't matter that you picked it up."

He blinks.

"It's just a shell. A dud." But we've both seen the other one explode. Still, I keep talking. "Moishe smashed the other one with a huge rock. This won't be like that. It'll be fine."

I take another step. David is five feet away. If the mortar blows now, we're both goners. I step closer and raise my hand, reaching for him.

"Give it to me," I say hoarsely. "We'll do it together."

David slowly moves a trembling hand. It's like in a dream, a nightmare, when you need to move fast but everything around you feels like thick syrup, holding you back. The cold metal touches my hand. It's heavier than it looks. My palm is so sweaty I'm scared I'll drop it.

"Slowly," I tell him, my voice still strangled. "Nice and easy."

David nods faintly. As if moving through water, we kneel together and gently, so gently, lay the mortar on the grassy dirt. It takes every ounce of my self-control not to flinch.

Nothing happens.

I nod. "Well done. Now step away." We're still alive.

David grips my hand tightly and slowly, carefully, steps away from the device. Our breaths saw in and out. The mortar remains inert in the grass.

We take another step back, then another, and then, as if our limbs have suddenly been unlocked, we run, our legs half buckling like noodles. We run and run, crying and laughing as we fly away on wings like eagles'.

"Motti!" My dad is running toward us. He's wearing a sweaty uniform, his hair disheveled. "Motti!" he shouts. "My boy!"

Shira is a few feet behind him.

"Abba!" I scream. "Abba!"

Now I'm really flying. I launch myself at him. He catches me in his strong arms, his chest solid under me. We're almost the same height. How have I not noticed that we are almost the same height?

My dad presses me against him. His prickly, unshaven jaw rubs against my face. I don't mind the scraping burn in the least.

"I can't believe you did that," he says, his voice thick with emotion. "I can't believe my son. When did you get so brave? My boy."

David has sunk to the ground, his legs unable to hold him. He's covered his face in his hands, shaking in relief.

"But I was so scared," I say, my face hidden in his shoulder. "I'm not brave. I'm not a hero. I could barely walk." I'm so disappointed in myself, I can taste the bitterness in my mouth.

"What are you talking about?" My dad pushes me away from him so he can see my face.

"You lost your favorite son." The words slip out before I can stop them. They sound so childish, but they're true. Gideon was the best of us.

I hang my head, unable to meet his eyes. "I'm no hero."

His grip on my shoulders tightens to the point of pain. "Look at me," he commands. He shakes hard enough to snap my neck up. "Look at me!"

His blue eyes are bloodshot and watery. He has deep bags under them. They're not even purple anymore. They're like bruises, nearly black. He looks ten years older than when I saw him yesterday.

"What I saw just now was one of the most extraordinary acts of bravery that I have ever seen. Motti, you almost killed me." He blinks rapidly. "I was so scared for you. But you did the right thing. You did it knowing it could cost you your life." For a second he loses the ability to speak. He takes a shaky breath and swallows heavily. "You did it to save your friend. You are the greatest, bravest boy I have ever met. *Because* you were scared. Because you did what had to be done *despite* that."

He pulls me toward him again and crushes me in his embrace. He shakes in my arms.

He's crying. My tough, strong dad is crying in my arms.

"I thought I was going to lose two of my boys today. Oh, God!" It's a prayer on his lips. "I am not strong enough for that."

So many feelings swirl inside me that for a moment, I can't even understand what I'm feeling. But finally it becomes clear. Love. I feel so full of love that my chest is tight and my limbs are warm. I'm alive. I love my dad. And I am so grateful for both of those things.

My dad lowers his head, shoulders bowed as if under a terrible weight. He closes his eyes, shuddering. After a moment, he visibly pulls himself together.

"Abba," I say. "It'll be okay." The same words that Gideon said to me the night before he returned to base. My brother was right about that, like he was about almost everything else.

"Abba?"

"Yes, Motti." His voice cracks. He brushes his tears away with a rough hand. "Yes, you're right. Come, your mom needs us to be with her." He keeps one hand around my shoulder and holds out the other hand to help David to his feet. "Let's get you home, David."

As I watch my dad struggle to hold himself together, to care for David, to keep me tucked safe under his arm, I remember what he told me before the war started. That there are all kinds of brave, all kinds of heroes. For the first time, his words make sense. In our own ways, all of us—my dad, my brothers, my mom, and maybe even me—have endured something that only the brave can face.

Chapter Nineteen
Mourning

The next evening at 6 p.m., a cease-fire goes into effect. The war is over. At 132 hours, it is one of the shortest wars in history. Egypt lost more than ten thousand men, 90 percent of its air force, and $2 billion worth of its military hardware. The Jordanians lost seven hundred men with six thousand wounded or missing. Syria lost more than four hundred men. In those same six days, the Israeli army lost eight hundred of its soldiers and 20 percent of its air force. But it also reclaimed the Old City, and unified Jerusalem.

Our apartment fills with relatives and friends who have come to sit shiva with us. Throughout the seven days of mourning, we'll sit at home while those who knew Gideon stop by to remember him. The mirrors are draped in black sheets. The kitchen is full of food. Everyone brings photos and stories about Gideon—from his excellent test scores to the Scouts he led, to the soldiers who served with him in his all-too-short military career. They hug my mom, they sit with my dad, they reminisce with Beni and me about Gideon's escapades.

The afternoon of our first day of mourning, my cousin runs to our mailbox and brings up the mail. She hands a stack of envelopes to my grandmother, who begins to sort through the bills and correspondence. She suddenly gives a small scream. All the conversations fall silent.

"What is it, Safta?" I ask. "What's wrong?"

My grandmother holds in her hand a light green military-issued envelope, the kind that soldiers use for personal correspondence. The address on the front is written in familiar handwriting. Gideon has sent us a letter.

He must have written it before the fighting started. With the chaos of the war, it took a while to reach us.

My mom gasps. She lifts the envelope to her nose, inhaling deeply, searching for a trace of her oldest son.

We crowd around the light green military-issued paper. My mom's hands shake a little as she opens it. It's as if Gideon has returned from the dead. I can't help but shiver. It feels like God has let my brother write to us from the other world.

With one hand placed over her trembling mouth, my mom reads the letter silently. Everyone in our crowded living room watches as she hands it to my dad. Beni and I stand waiting. Though my soul shakes with the desire to read it, I wait patiently as my dad reads, then rereads, the tidy handwritten lines, blinking his red-rimmed eyes fiercely. Then he hands it to me and Beni. We stand side by side, reading it together.

To my dear parents: Our commander has told all of us to take a moment and write down a few lines to our family. He says it isn't in case we die, but so that we're clear about what we're fighting for. I think he's right. Not that any of us forget for a moment we're fighting for our lives and our families, but it's good for you to be at the front of my mind as we head out.

I don't think anything bad will happen to me. I hope that we will all see each other again. But in case we don't, I want you to know how much I love you. I count being your son as my greatest blessing. You taught me about honor and hard work, and everything I am today is because of you.

To Motti: I know that I am sometimes hard on you. I tease you. I push you. But it's only because I see how special you are. Smart, quick, funny. Great things are in store for you. If for some reason I don't come back from this, I'm still with you. I'm still your big brother, and I'll be there with you no matter what comes. Listen to Mom and Dad. Take care of Beni. I love you.

To Beni: I'll never forget seeing your little face for the first time. I was twelve years old. Mom gave me this little bundle all wrapped in a blanket. Only your red face was peeking out.

I just lost my heart. You and Motti are the best brothers that I could ever hope for. Listen to Mom and Dad. Don't be too hard on Motti. I love you and I'm with you no matter what.

All my love,

Gideon

Beni is a slower reader than I am, so I hold the letter steady, waiting until he finishes. When he nods, I hand the letter back to my parents, who immediately reread the precious lines. My mother's lips move as she looks at the words, probably hearing them said in Gideon's voice. Beni leans his head against my chest as we watch them. I put my arms around his narrow shoulders, Gideon's last words echoing in my mind.

Soon the letter is passed from person to person—to my aunts and uncles and grandparents. Gideon's message makes everyone cry.

A choking sadness fills me. It hits me once more that I'll never see Gideon again. We'll never have another letter from him. I'll never see his half-smile before he makes a joke, or the true smile that fills his face when he makes us laugh. I'll never hear any more of the interesting ideas that he shared or be able to turn to him for advice. All gone. Forever.

I'm desperate to get away from the well-meaning crowd. Swallowing back the tears gags me. I don't want to upset my parents with more crying, so I slip out the front door, stepping lightly down the dim staircase.

I have half-formed plans of walking to the stadium. But as soon as I'm out of the building, I find Mrs. Friedburg sitting on the front stoop. I almost don't recognize her. The always impeccably dressed lady who spent a night in a bomb shelter without a hair out of place has her dress buttoned wrong at the collar. Her hair is unkempt. Instantly, I know she's lost someone she loves too. She is a woman in mourning.

"Who did you lose, Mrs. Friedburg?" I ask, kneeling next to her.

She looks at me in shock. "Who did I lose? I lost Gideon. I lost our Gideon. That beautiful boy."

Now that the rest of my family has come to our apartment to keep my parents from sinking into despair, Mrs. Friedburg has fallen to pieces. She covers her face with her hands, weeping. I feel helpless to comfort her when my own grief chokes me. But she pulls me into her arms, hugging me tightly. I don't swallow back the tears anymore. We cry and cry, mourning our loss together.

* * *

In the days following the end of the war, the grandest sense of euphoria sweeps through Jerusalem and the entire country. When a stranger passing us on the street pulls my mom into a big hug and kisses her cheeks, my parents and I hardly blink. Everywhere strangers embrace each other, feeling like one family. For the first time in two millennia the Jewish people have fought, have won, and have united the city that lies at the heart of our religious identity. Some Holocaust survivors, like our neighbor Mr. Pinsky, say that with this, they have finally forgiven God for what they endured.

The days pass in a blurry daze. There are moments when I forget that Gideon died. I automatically think about telling him something, and then with a bitter, painful jolt, I remember. He's gone. It makes me wonder how Mrs. Friedburg survived losing her whole family. How any of those Holocaust survivors found the strength to move past their grief. Maybe I will too one day. I don't know.

The Wall

When I think back on that summer in 1967, I have a clear, vibrant memory of the first time I saw the Western Wall.

After we finished sitting shiva for Gideon, we went to the Old City.

My parents, Beni, and I, the four of us, joined thousands of other Jews, crying, laughing, cheering, carried along toward the holiest of holies. I walked on cobbled alleys that had seen three thousand years of passing feet. The Jordanians who lived there came out to meet us. They waved and smiled as we passed. Children approached us, smiling shyly and holding trays with key chains and necklaces for sale.

Many people bought their goods, excited to be interacting with Jordanians for the first time in twenty years. It seemed as if, even though they'd lost the war, they were interested in us—curious about us. Maybe they were just pretending, but at that moment, I believed that they wanted to live in peace, just like us.

We avoided passing by the YMCA, the Alley of Death that took Gideon. Instead, we wound our way through the narrow, twisting streets. And suddenly, it was there in front of us. The tall, white wall that I had only seen in illustrations and photos. Each stone was massive, taller than a man, wider than a car. How the builders had moved such mammoth boulders two thousand years ago was beyond my understanding.

My mom and dad held hands as they approached. Later there would be a partition separating men from women. But in those first heady days after the war, there was nothing to divide the tens of thousands of people who came to touch, to pray, to see with their own eyes the miracle of a unified Jerusalem.

I remember my mom shaking, tears running unchecked down her face. I held onto Beni's hand so we wouldn't lose him in the massive crowd around us.

We approached the wall. It was so serene, unmoved by the struggle and the cost we had paid to come see it.

I touched a massive ancient stone, worn smooth. Someone next to me whispered the *Shehechiyanu* under his breath, a prayer of gratitude for experiencing something for the first time. But I didn't want to say the *Shehechiyanu.*

Instead, I leaned my forehead against the pale wall of Jerusalem stone and said the *Kaddish*, the prayer for mourning.

At first it was only me saying it.

Then my parents' voices joined in, and Beni's. Then the man who had chanted *Shehechiyanu* added his voice. Then the couple next to him echoed our solemn prayer for the dead.

Because, as the soldier who had come to my door had said, we were not the only ones who had lost someone dear. In our small country, losing eight hundred young men was a hard blow. The whole nation was both celebrating and mourning. So more and more voices joined our *Kaddish*. Until the thousands of people who had come to the Western Wall chanted as one, our voices rumbling in the square, rising higher and higher. A prayer of sadness and hope, grief and faith.

Then we all said, "Amen."

* * *

Afterward, my father said, "Come, let me show you where I used to live."

We followed him through the ancient, narrow streets. The buildings were so close to each other that unless it was high noon, the sun couldn't reach the street. My dad walked briskly through the shadowy lanes, confident of his way even though he hadn't set foot there in nearly twenty years.

Beni and I swiveled our heads from side to side, trying to take it all in. Many Jordanians had tied white shirts or scarfs to their balconies and front doors, to let the Israeli soldiers know they had surrendered. People came out of their apartments and stood by their homes as we walked by. They smiled at us, waving.

"*Ahlan*," my dad would say as we passed. "*As-salamu 'alaykum*."

"*Wa 'alaykum*," someone would say back.

Beni and I exchanged googly eyes. Abba spoke Arabic?

We walked for ten minutes before arriving at a plain white building with a heavy, ancient-looking wooden door.

"This was my house," my dad said, sounding far away. "We lived on the second floor, my grandparents were on the first floor, and my aunt and uncle lived on the third floor." He cleared his throat violently. My mom took his hand in hers. We all gazed at the scarred door. I tried to picture my dad as a young boy, scampering in and out of this building, running through these twisting, maze-like streets. What a different life he had lived.

"Where did your friend Daoud live?" I asked.

He blinked rapidly, as if waking from a dream. "Not far." He smiled. "Let me show you."

We walked for a few more minutes. Though I couldn't tell the difference, my dad said we had left the Jewish Quarter and were now in the Muslim Quarter. A few streets away was a plain, three-story building, almost identical to the one my father grew up in, except for a wrought iron door decorated in curves and loops.

We stood there looking at the little house, not sure what to do.

Men in long white robes and head dresses passed us, eyeing us with uncertainty. Women wearing long black robes hurried by with heavy bags of groceries in their arms. We stood out in our shorts and sandals.

I thought about how my dad had said good-bye to his childhood friend nineteen years ago—probably the same way I'd said good-bye to Yossi. I didn't know if I'd ever see Yossi again. I hoped so. I hoped his mother would be able to believe in Israel again. But if not . . . maybe nineteen years from now, I'd be in my dad's position. Staring at Yossi's old house, wondering what had happened to him.

"Maybe he still lives here," I said. "You should knock." My dad rapped against the door frame.

We waited and waited.

"Maybe they're not home," Beni said. And then we heard it, the turn of an old bolt. The inner door opened, and through the iron curves we saw a slim, middle-aged man with thinning hair. He had a worried look on his face that turned into puzzlement when he saw an Israeli family standing at his doorway.

"Yes?" he asked in Hebrew.

"Excuse me. Is there a man named Daoud who lives here?"

"Yes," he said, his puzzlement growing. "I am Daoud."

"I am Avner," my dad said. "Do you remember me? It's been a long time."

Daoud's face grew brighter and brighter as he fit the memory of his childhood friend over the older face of my dad standing in front of him.

"Avner!" he cried. "My old friend! I can't believe it!"

He fumbled with the lock on the iron gate as he shouted something in rapid Arabic over his shoulder.

"Come in! Come in! I can't believe this!"

The door swung open and the two men fell into a hug, swaying back and forth. Daoud touched my dad's face, laughing in disbelief over the wrinkles. My dad teased him about the thinning hair.

A woman wearing a colorful headscarf came from the back of the house, wiping her hands on a towel.

She said something in Arabic, and none of us needed to speak the language to know she was welcoming us inside. The four of us entered the home of my father's childhood friend.

Two girls and a young boy were inside, playing with a model train set. They froze at the sight of us. Beni and I edged closer to each other. The parents shooed us toward one another.

Before I knew it, a plate of cookies was put on a low end table and cups of sweet mint tea were poured for everyone.

The adults sat and talked for an hour. Daoud

had lost his brother in the war. His parents' new house had been destroyed. My parents told him about Gideon. I looked at them, the two sets of parents, and for one disorienting moment I couldn't see the difference between them. Why had we fought each other? Why had we lost loved ones?

For one shining, hopeful afternoon, I thought it was over. That we would all live in peace. That we would all be friends.

And why not? My family and I had just prayed at the Western Wall. We had scrawled little prayers on scraps of paper and stuffed them into the small spaces between the massive stones. There is a belief that prayers left at the wall will find their way to God's ear. Thousands of slips of paper daily. Hundreds of thousands of prayers. And I think most of them are prayers for peace.

As Daoud and my father filled each other in on the past nineteen years of their lives, I thought, *Why not peace?*

Anything was possible.

Author's Note

My father was an eighteen-year-old university student in Israel when the Six-Day War broke out in 1967. His parents were Holocaust survivors, scarred and wary of the evil in the world. They had barely escaped Europe with their lives. But my dad—a bright, ambitious young man who had lived in Israel since he was a toddler—was untroubled by history's shadow. He scoffed at his dad's worries of doom and destruction.

Everything changed in May 1967, when Egyptian president Gamal Abdel Nasser moved large armies into the desert. He demanded the United Nations leave Sinai, and they complied. President Nasser moved cannons to the southern tip of the Sinai, blocking the Straits of Tiran to

Israeli ships sailing to Israel. As Egypt amassed troops on its southern border, Syrian forces to the north went on high alert. Then Jordan, bordering Israel in the south and east, signed a treaty putting its military under Egyptian control.

Within weeks, Israel was surrounded by powerful enemies, its military outnumbered five to one. As fears grew in Israel, my dad suddenly respected his father's worldview. If his young country couldn't stop its enemies, no one else would either.

But unlike in the Second World War, this time the Jewish people had a military and a plan. The Israeli military destroyed the air forces of three nations in about six hours. It changed the course of the war and of history.

Acknowledgments

Many people helped me with this book. I wish to thank my parents, particularly my father, Gabriel Laufer, for sharing so vividly his experiences as an eighteen-year-old Israeli soldier in the Six-Day War. My aunt and uncle, Sara and Rafi Kornfeld, told me about their experiences as a young nurse (Sara) and soldier (Rafi) during that time. Sara and Yaakov Hassidim were children living in West Jerusalem, and their terrific descriptions of daily life, as well as of the dangers and drama of the Six-Day War, helped shape my vision of what it must have been like to live then. Mickey Obed, an activated soldier in the reserves, survived in a unit that took terrible losses in heavy fighting. He helped me understand what was happening on the front lines during the war. Katherine Janus Kahn was an American volunteer in Israel in 1967. She generously shared with me what the national mood was like and what inspired young men and women from around the world to come help a struggling, war-torn country.

Yetnayet Lemma made sure the details of Motti's encounter with the Ethiopian priest were factually accurate. Any errors are my own.

I found the true story of Yoni Netanyahu particularly inspiring as I developed Gideon's character. Yoni was a bright, talented young man who chose to dedicate himself to Israel's defense and security at the cost of his own future. He served honorably and bravely in the Six-Day War and the Yom Kippur War, and died leading a successful rescue operation to save a plane full of passengers kidnapped by terrorists. To find out more about him, I recommend watching the documentary about his life, *Follow Me: The Yoni Netanyahu Story.*

While I read many books and articles about the Six-Day War, Michael Oren's fantastic book

Six Days of War: June 1967 and the Making of the Modern Middle East was incredibly valuable in helping me grasp the terror that preceded the war and the giddy relief that followed.

Thank you to fellow authors Caroline Hickey and Kristin Levine, who gave spot-on comments and suggestions that made this book better on a tight deadline.

A final thank you goes to Harold Grinspoon, who founded the PJ Library, a program dedicated to mailing free, high-quality children's books about Jewish life to Jewish families.